REBEL
McKenzie

REBEL McKENZIE

CANDICE RANSOM

SCHOLASTIC INC.

ISBN 978-0-545-60415-4

12 11 10 9 8 7 6 5 4 3 2 1   14 15 16 17 18/0

Printed in the U.S.A.   40

First Scholastic printing, May 2013

This book is set in Garamond MT.
Designed by Marci Senders

Publisher's Note: The recipes contained in this book are to be followed exactly as written, under adult supervision. The Publisher is not responsible for your specific health or allergy needs that may require medical supervision. The Publisher is not responsible for any adverse reactions to the recipes contained in this book.

For my sister Patricia,
hot dog spaghetti chef and hairdresser extraordinaire

REBEL
McKenzie

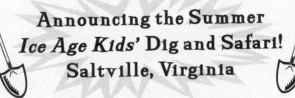

Announcing the Summer
Ice Age Kids' Dig and Safari!
Saltville, Virginia

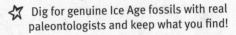

☆ Dig for genuine Ice Age fossils with real paleontologists and keep what you find!

 ☆ Identify and prepare fossils!

☆ Build a model of a Saber-toothed Cat to keep!

☆ Go on a Megalodon Shark's Tooth Hunt and keep one giant shark's tooth!

 ☆ Field trips to footprint sites!

☆ Special Ice Age breakfasts! Mastodon Sausage, Bison Bacon, Great Bear Grits, Giant Beaver Biscuits, and Paleo Pancakes!

☆ Toast marshmallows and sing around the campfire!

Spend one adventure-packed week in Saltville, where fossils of Ice Age mammals and human artifacts (from 14,000 years ago!) are preserved in the time line of blue-gray clay that dates back more than 200,000 years!

Fee includes meals, lodging (authentic log cabins!), and field supplies. Register early!

 Dig #1: June 21–28
Dig #2: August 8–15

ONE

Never Wear Seven Pairs
of Underpants

Convicts can spot a runaway right off the stick. I found that out too late.

I was trudging down Coolbrook Road, a big fat lie of a name if there ever was one. The brook was invisible, unless you counted the dried-up gulley running alongside. And I would have had to catch on fire first to cool off.

It was late afternoon. I'd missed the stupid once-a-day Greyhound by hours, but staggered on before vultures circled. A five-hundred-degree sun sizzled overhead. I was so thirsty, the back of my throat felt peeled, like paint off an old barn. I would have killed—absolutely *killed*—for a blueberry Slurpee.

"Runnin' away, girlie?" said a soft voice. I looked up.

A man hefted a shovelful of leaves and dirt. He wore a navy blue jumpsuit with a loose orange vest, like a highway worker.

"I run off oncet." He grinned, showing crooked dark-brown teeth. "See where it got me. Cleanin' ditches with a bunch of jailbirds."

Down the road, men in the same outfits scraped leaves and trash out of the gulley. A guard with a rifle leaned against the fender of a white bus with grilled windows.

My heart bumped. I had walked smack into a road gang.

"I'm not running away," I said, only partly lying. "I'm . . . out for a walk."

"Wearin' half your clothes? You look swolled up like a tick."

It was true I had on seven pairs of underwear, four pairs of shorts, and five T-shirts, another reason I was about to spontaneously combust. The rest of my earthly possessions were crammed in the big straw purse slung over my shoulder.

"You shouldn't make fun of chubby people," I said, sounding offended. "What did you do to land in jail? Rob a bank?"

"Your face is red as a pepper pod, and I bet you got blisters the size of cow pies in them flimsy tennis shoes. You're a runaway, all right."

How did he know so much?

All morning I had cleverly snuck down back roads, figuring the police would patrol the main highway. I stopped only once after crossing the old Bull Run Bridge, to dip my sore feet in the river. The water was muddy and warm as a birdbath. When I pulled my feet out, dozens of tiny black suckers clung to my ankles.

I smacked the leeches off, trying not to faint from sheer gross-outedness. Then I slipped my sweaty sneakers back on and hobbled down the road.

"Take my advice," the convict said. "Go home and quit worryin' your mama."

"I'm not running *away*," I said to set him straight. "I'm going *to* someplace."

"Uh-huh."

"I signed up for the Ice Age Kids' Dig in Saltville, and my mother said, 'We'll see.' Sometimes her 'we'll sees' actually mean yes." I shifted my purse to the other shoulder. "But our fridge croaked, and Mama said *our* ice age problem was more important and she didn't have the money to send me."

"So you're goin' anyways. Do you know how far Saltville is? Clear on the edge of yonder."

"I was going to take the Greyhound from Red Onion with the rest of my birthday money." Ten dollars should buy my ticket, I figured. "But I missed the bus."

"It's a fair piece from Frog Level to Red Onion. A good eight miles."

"I have work to do," I said. "I'm a paleontologist."

"A what?" The convict leaned on his shovel.

"A scientist who 'specializes in reading the record of

past life in rocks,'" I quoted from *The How and Why Wonder Book of Prehistoric Mammals*. "'Understanding the past is crucial to understanding the present.'"

The convict scratched his nose. "I reckon."

Just then the guard glanced in our direction and gripped his rifle.

"Skeeter!" the guard barked. "No talking to civilians! You, girl, get a move on."

Skeeter dropped into the ditch. "Bet you're nabbed within the hour."

"Bet I'm not," I said. "I've dodged the cops all day."

"Twenty bucks?"

"You're on!" I leaned over the ditch. "How will I know where to find you? To collect my money?"

He grinned up at me. "You can send *my* money to Red Onion Correctional Unit. Eighteen hundred Ray of Hope Lane. I won't be goin' nowhere soon."

I hitched up my purse and headed down the road. The guard gave me hard eyes as I sidled by.

"Visiting my grandma," I said, making out I was Little Red Riding Hood. "You have a nice day, now."

Skeeter won the bet.

A half-dead fly bumbled behind my Venetian blinds. I was flat on my back in bed, my knees propped on a pillow so my heels wouldn't touch the mattress. Mid-afternoon sun sifted through the blinds. I lay still as a lizard, with Tusky, my faithful stuffed mammoth, at my side. I didn't intend to ever move again.

My door opened. I glared at the intruder. "Doesn't anyone ever *knock*?"

Mama bustled in. "Don't take that tone with me, missy. I didn't tell you to run off and get your feet in this sorry state."

The policeman alerted by that blabbermouth convict guard had picked me up and brought me home three days ago. Mama had shrieked at the sight of my blood-caked tennis shoes. I soaked my feet in the tub while she gently tweezed gravel from my blisters. Then we went to the doctor. He prescribed a special ointment and antibiotics.

Mama pried one corner of the bandage from my right foot. "The infection looks better already. But you were an inch away from gangrene, you know that?" She picked up the tube of ointment on my dresser.

"You remind me every five minutes." I winced as she applied the ointment.

"The doctor says you'll have scars. And forget about closed-back shoes." She smoothed a new bandage over each heel.

"Who cares about shoes? Who cares about anything?"

My whole summer was ruined. Mama and Daddy had grounded me the rest of my born days for worrying them to a frazzle. I would never go on a field dig with real paleontologists or eat Bison Bacon (not real bison) and

Ground Sloth Gravy (not real ground sloth) or listen to stories about the Ice Age around a campfire.

I wanted to excavate a woolly mammoth skeleton and stake my place in paleontology history. I'd be famous, like that English girl who found a dinosaur skeleton in a cliff a long time ago. Instead I was stuck in podunky Frog Level, doomed to wear bedroom slippers until I graduated from college.

Mama plucked bandage wrappers from the chenille counterpane. "You did this to yourself, Rebel. If you had told us you wanted to go to camp that bad, we would have worked something out."

"I *did* tell you! But the new refrigerator was more important! Everything is more important than me!" Tears stung my eyes.

She pressed the back of her hand against my forehead like she had when I was a little kid. "No fever. You've been cooped up in this room too long. Come on out."

"Don't feel like it."

She tidied my dresser. "I'm fixing potato soup and corn fritters. Your favorites."

"Not hungry."

With a sigh, Mama left, cracking the door open.

The brochure for the Kids' Dig was thumbtacked to the bulletin board over my dresser. The picture showed excited-looking kids tucking into Paleo Pancakes and Mastodon Sausage, stoking up before a day in the field.

I'd miss the June Kids' Dig. No chance of getting to the August one, either. I might as well be trapped in the blue-gray clay with the Saltville Ice Age animals.

The fly threw itself futilely at the window. I fell asleep, my face buried in Tusky's worn fur.

"She pulled this stunt just to get attention."

A familiar voice woke me up.

"Now she's laying in there like the Queen of Sheba so you can wait on her."

My mother's voice drifted from the living room. "Rebel is high-strung. Both you girls are. I don't know why I didn't have boys. They aren't nearly as worrisome."

"I never caused you half the trouble Rebel does, and you threatened to send *me* to reform school. One time you even got my suitcase down from the attic, remember? Maybe Rebel needs a dose of reform school."

I sat up. The person who wanted Mama to ship me away was my older sister. I slipped off the rumpled counterpane and limped into the living room.

Lynette sat on the sofa across from Mama, twisting a piece of her blond hair. Her orange lipstick and fingernail and toenail polish matched her miniskirt. She looked like an ad for Florida orange juice.

Pasted by her side was a spindly-legged boy with cowlicky brown hair and a narrow, ferret face. His skin was so pale, I could see veins pulsing in his temples. He put me in

9

mind of one of those plants that grow under rocks.

My nephew, Rudy.

I'd been an aunt since I was five, which had always felt weird. I hadn't seen my sister or Rudy for three years. They were forever moving. Ohio. Tennessee. Kentucky.

"When did you get here?" I asked Lynette, slumping in the rocking chair. "And since when are you a blonde?"

"Day before yesterday and since yesterday," she replied. "Nice to see you too."

"Lynette's back for good," Mama said. "She's renting in Grandview Estates."

"Really?" I said. "Great. I guess. But where's Chuck going to race his monster truck? I thought that's why y'all left Frog Level in the first place."

Lynette's shoulders stiffened. "Rebel, say hi to Rudy. It's been donkey's years since you saw him last. You're a big boy now, aren't you, Poopsy Poodle?"

"Hey, Rudy," I said. "How old are you? Fifteen? Sixteen?"

"Aw, Rebel. I'm only seven." He pronounced it "seben."

He grinned, showing one front tooth, big as a billboard. The other tooth stuck straight out like an opened garage door. Adhesive-taped glasses slid down his pug nose. He knuckled them back in place.

"Where's Chuck?" I asked.

"Last I heard, still in Alabama."

"Daddy's racing Mud Hog this weekend," Rudy put in.

"Just like he does every weekend." Lynette flicked her hair behind one ear. "I'm tired of playing second fiddle to a truck on growth hormones. So I packed up Rudy and came back to Virginia."

I knew my brother-in-law always wanted to be a NASCAR driver. He flunked pit crew because he couldn't change tires fast enough or something. Then Chuck bought himself a monster truck. He raced Mud Hog in county fairs and monster jams, which never sounded like much of a job to me.

"What are your plans?" Mama asked Lynette.

"I enrolled in Dot's Pink Palace Beauty Academy. Everybody says I'm good with hair. I have to stand on my own two feet since I can't put no depends in Chuck. I have to think of Rudy."

"Beauty school is fine, but it won't put bread on the table," Mama said.

"I also got a job as a shampoo girl. And Chuck will send money. But I can't leave Rudy all day while I'm at school in the morning and Hair Magic in the afternoons." Lynette turned to me. "That's where you come in, Rebel."

"Me?"

"A lady a few mobile homes down keeps an eye on the neighborhood kids, but she's not a full-time babysitter," my sister replied. "I need you to live with us this summer and watch Rudy."

Mama shook her head. "Rebel's too young—"

"She's twelve!" Lynette insisted. "Time she had some responsibility. Instead of worrying you with her foolish notions, let her *work*."

"I don't know," Mama said, weakening just the slightest. "Rebel's young for her age."

"I am not!" I was a paleontologist, practically.

"Mama, this will be *good* for Rebel."

"Do *I* have any say in this?" I asked the air.

Mama stood. "I'll call your daddy and see what he thinks." She went into the kitchen.

"If I do this—" I said to my sister. "*If* . . . how much will you pay me?" I might swing that second Kids' Dig trip after all.

"Nothing," Lynette said bluntly. "I can't afford it."

"I'm not going to work for nothing! That's slavery!"

Mama came back. "Okay, Rebel, your daddy says you can go. Lynette, make sure she uses that cream and changes her bandages."

"I'm not going!" I yelled. "She's not paying me one red cent!"

"You are going," Mama said. "Your sister needs you."

What choice did I have? It was either go to Lynette's or rot in my bedroom.

While Mama slapped clothes in my duffel bags, suddenly eager to get rid of me, Rudy told me more about their trailer.

"Our new house came with two surprises," he said. "A bed filled with water!"

"The water bed is nice," Lynette said. "The cat is not."

"His name is Doublewide, and he's the fattest cat I've ever seen! He can do tricks!" Rudy's eyebrows nearly leaped into his hairline.

"Like what?" I asked.

Lynette's mouth twisted. "He tee-tees in the toilet. And he rings the doorbell when he wants to come in."

"You're kidding. Who would train a cat to pee in the toilet?"

Lynette shrugged. "Saves on kitty litter."

"Doublewide acts just like a person!" Rudy bounced on the sofa cushion.

"Honeybunch, we don't jump on furniture," Lynette said, tapping his knee. "That cat is so smart, he's creepy. But we have to keep him. He's part of the rental deal."

Mama lugged two stuffed duffel bags to the door. "I think this is everything."

"Rebel can always *wear* the rest of her clothes," Lynette said with a smirk.

"Ha-ha."

I packed my paleontology equipment: geologist's hammer, putty knife, trowel, soft paintbrushes, field notebook, magnifying glass. Even though I was in exile this summer, I could still hunt for fossils.

I tucked Tusky and *The How and Why Wonder Book of*

Prehistoric Mammals in my backpack. I was ready.

Lynette piled my bags in the trunk of an old clunker. "If Chuck knew I was driving this, he'd have forty heart attacks. I traded in his sports car—which I needed like another hole in the head—for this. Ain't pretty, but it runs."

The vinyl passenger seat was crisscrossed with frayed duct tape. I got in, screaming, "Oooch, eeech, ouch!" The seat was scalding, and the duct tape pinched my thighs.

Mama leaned in the window to kiss my cheek. "Behave, now, Rebel. Your daddy and I will miss you. Lynette, be sure to look after Rebel's heels. And don't let her stay up too late."

"Don't worry, Mama."

Lynette started the car and backed it down the driveway. Mama waved in obvious relief. I felt like a baton handed off in a relay race.

As we drove out of town (*You Are Leaving Frog Level, Incorporated 1903, Population 39 Plus 18 Dogs*), Lynette chattered about her new life.

"I can't wait to start beauty school! But I'm a little nervous too. You'll help me with my homework, won't you, Rebel?"

"Sure." I glanced in the backseat. Rudy was studying one of Lynette's fashion magazines scattered on the floorboard. What a funny little kid he was.

Lynette switched on the radio. "Rudy is just an Angel Mae. You won't have a bit of trouble. But he's such a picky eater. I wish you'd get him to eat better."

"What does he eat?" I asked. I wasn't planning on doing a lot of cooking.

"Every morning, he has an RC float. He won't touch a crumb except hot dog spaghetti for lunch and dinner—"

"*What* kind of spaghetti?"

"It's a breeze to fix. You take cooked spaghetti and add some ketchup and a little sugar. Then fry a couple of hot dogs, cut up like pennies, you know? Stir it all up. Sometimes you can throw in a small can of peas."

Dis*gust*ing. "That's *all* he eats?"

"And cookies. You see why I'm trying to broaden his tastes." She glanced in the rearview mirror. "Put some meat on his bird bones. Ain't that right, Rudykins?"

Rudy sat forward with his magazine. He pointed to a navy blue dress trimmed in white lace.

"Do you like this?" he asked me. "I bet you'd look nice in it."

I shrugged. I didn't bother much about clothes. "It's okay."

"I'll mark the page," he said, settling back again. "This is the dress you'll be laid out in."

"Say what?" I stared at my sister. "What in Sam Hill is he talking about?"

"Nothing. He went to his grandmother Parsley's

funeral last month and picked up some notions. That's all." She turned the radio up louder.

That's all? My Angel Mae nephew shopped for people's funeral outfits before they were even dead. What *else* had Lynette conveniently forgotten to tell me?

From the Field Notebook of Rebel McKenzie

I have found a missing link! My *How and Why Wonder Book of Prehistoric Mammals* says that Thomas Jefferson had some bones from a cave in Virginia. The bones were from a strange animal. Thomas Jefferson called the animal a *Megalonyx*—a gigantic prehistoric lion he thought was still roaming the wild forests of the West.

Scientists later figured out Jefferson's bones were from a huge ground sloth. They named it *Megalonyx jeffersonii* because Jefferson discovered it.

My book says, "The Megalonyx was a huge, hairy animal that walked on the sides of its four long-clawed feet. It had a thick hairy tail upon which it could rest some of its weight when it stood on its hind legs to browse on leaves high up in the trees." Some ground sloths were over six feet tall and weighed 3,500 pounds!

When I get to the Kids' Dig, I'm going to tell the paleontologists that I have discovered the direct descendant of *Megalonyx*. Thomas Jefferson was almost right—a smaller version of his strange lion animal is right here in Virginia.

I am naming it *Megalonyx doublewideus*.

TWO

Doublewide, the Wonder Cat

Grandview Estates was anything but. Not grand. Not an estate. And the only view was of a giant sewer pipe rising from a scraggy vacant lot.

"Hey, you got a 7-Eleven in your trailer park," I said as we passed a small strip shopping center. "Can we stop for a blueberry Slurpee?"

"Not now. And don't say trailer park," Lynette corrected. "We live in a *mobile home community*."

"Pardon *moi*," I said, slouching down to dangle my bare feet out the window.

"Sit right. Only trash ride down the road like that."

I pulled my feet in and folded my arms across my chest. Lynette acted like a prissy old lady. *Don't say trailer park. Only trash stick their feet out the car window.* She *was* old—twenty-six, fourteen years older than me. She married Charles

Parsley and left home when I was just four. I really didn't know her very well. What if I'd traded one mother for another? The thought hardly filled my heart with gladness.

I looked out at the *mobile homes* lining the streets end-wise. Double-wides and single-wides all claimed tiny yards, some overgrown with weeds, others so neat they could have been clipped with manicure scissors. The better-kept lawns had white-washed tires blooming with petunias and baskets of geraniums hanging from awnings.

Some trailers boasted screen porches or carports and freshly painted trim. But a lot of them looked neglected. We drove by trailers with crooked Venetian blinds, busted barbecue grills, and bent TV antennas.

Noticing stuff was part of my training. Paleontologists have to be keen observers, because most people aren't. A rock an ordinary person would kick aside could turn out to be the toe bone of a giant Ice Age beaver. You never knew.

I stared at a white trailer with ceramic cat figurines crawling up its shutters. Orange, red, and pink zinnias rocketed from the picket-fenced yard. A green cement frog squatted in a birdbath. The grass was as green as Oz.

"That's Miz Matthews's place," Lynette remarked. "She watches the kids on our street sometimes."

"Yesterday she gave me a quarter for the vending machines at the firehouse." Rudy's bony arm stretched over the back of the seat as he pointed to a brick building.

"They have soda machines and candy machines and ones with potato chips—"

Junk food within walking distance. That was promising.

"Miz Matthews kept an eye on Rudy so I could enroll in Dot's Pink Palace Beauty Academy." Lynette wheeled The Clunker into a short driveway, parked under a tottering metal carport, and switched off the engine. The car coughed like an old man clearing his throat, then sputtered into silence.

"We'll come back for your things in a minute," Lynette said to me.

Her yard was summer-fried, brown and crispy as a taco. Sun-starched towels, T-shirts, and denim cutoffs hung stiffly from an umbrella clothespole. I climbed out of the car barefoot and tromped on crabgrass sharp as knife blades.

"Yow!" I yelled, hopping into my flip-flops. Heat baked through the rubber bottoms. Apparently, Grandview Estates was built on a volcano.

Lynette frowned. "Keep your shoes on, dummy."

"Hey!" Rudy cried. "There's Doublewide!"

A large, dark-brown blob perched on a rusted patio table by the front door. It unwound a whiplike tail from around dainty front paws and arched its back. The cat was shaped like a chocolate-colored basketball with a smaller ball balanced on top. His face and ears were nearly black and his coat was sleek as a seal's.

Crossed blue eyes watched us. When we were nearly at the door, the cat stood on its hind legs, reached up with one paw, and whacked the doorbell. *Ding-dong*. I heard the faint chime inside.

"We're right *here*," my sister told the cat, fumbling with her keys. "You don't have to ring."

"He does that all the time?" I asked. "That's so cool!"

"The first few times we heard the doorbell, we thought it was kids messing around. Then I looked out and saw this stupid cat, big as life, hitting the button."

"Doublewide is real smart. He could be on TV." Rudy stroked the cat's head. "He's a Siamese!" He pronounced it "Si-meeze."

Lynette unlocked the door and Doublewide streaked in ahead of her. "But not a purebreed. He's got a kink in his tail and his eyes are crossed. Plus he weighs twenty-one pounds. You can hear his thighs rub together when he walks. Siamese are supposed to be slinky."

"You could use him for a footstool," I said, and Rudy giggled.

"I could use him for a garbage disposal," Lynette said. "He eats like a Saint Bernard. I'd get rid of the big pest, but he's part of the lease. The owner moved to an apartment that doesn't allow pets."

"How would he know if you got rid of Doublewide?" I asked.

"That cat would probably call social services on me."

We walked into a little hall. The kitchen was
side. I spied a bedroom on the other. Two steps dov
hall and we were in the living room.

"The movers delivered our furniture yesterday,"
Lynette said. "I left Chuck his tacky recliner and the patio
chairs. No way is he getting the Spanish modern living
room suite I worked my tail off at Ben Franklin to pay
for."

I didn't know Spanish modern from a hole in the
ground, but Lynette's living room made a funeral parlor
look like a carnival. Low-slung black vinyl chairs skulked
around the walls. A red glass globe lamp swung from a
thick brass chain. A painting of a bullfighter on black velvet in a fancy gold frame hung over the black sofa.

"I still have to put up the drapes," Lynette said, "and
then our place will be all nice and cozy."

I'd seen cozier dungeons.

She showed me the rest of the trailer, which took about
three minutes. Down another hall were a little blue-tiled
bathroom and Lynette's room with a water bed smack in
the middle of the green shag carpet. I threw myself on the
water bed. Waves sloshed me back and forth.

"I'd get seasick in that thing," I said, struggling to
clamber off. "How do you sleep in it?"

"You're not supposed to jump in like a pearl diver."

Rudy's bedroom was at the far end of the trailer, opposite the kitchen. His room was so small, I had to mince

sideways between the sway-backed twin beds.

"That one's yours," Rudy said, generously giving me the bed half-blocked by a dresser. Going to the bathroom in the middle of the night should be tons of fun. I wondered where I could buy shin guards.

"Why is it so hot in here?" I asked, pushing my bangs off my forehead.

"The A/C is on the fritz," Lynette answered. "Let's bring your bags in so you can get settled. Then I'll fix supper."

On the way out, the phone in the kitchen rang. Lynette grabbed the receiver.

"Hi, Mama. Yeah, we just got in. . . . What did you forget? . . . You're *kidding* me. Okay, catch y'all later."

"What did Mama want?" I asked.

"To make sure your feet were okay, for one. I didn't tell her you were prancing around barefoot. She also told me to hold your hand when we cross the street."

"*What*? I'm *twelve*, for Pete's sake!"

"According to Mama, you never look where you're going and you're liable to get run over. Rudy must take after you. He trips over dust. His glasses are taped because he falls and breaks them all the time."

"You are *not* holding my hand to cross the street," I said, bristling. "I look down at the ground because I might miss an important fossil."

"Uh-huh." She sounded just like Mama—not really

interested in what *I'm* interested in.

There was no place in Rudy's room to put my things. Superhero comics were stacked on his nightstand. His dresser was packed with clothes and blankets. Rows of little NASCAR model cars lined the dresser top, surrounded by plastic cups advertising monster truck rallies.

"My daddy give me these," Rudy said, rolling a red car to the edge of the dresser. "I'm gonna be a race car driver someday."

"Has your daddy ever won a race in his monster truck?"

I plumped Tusky at the foot of my bed, then stacked my clothes on the closet shelf. Doublewide lounged against my pillow, taking a brisk bath.

"Not yet, but he will," Rudy replied. "Mud Hog is the baddest truck of all!"

Mud Hog couldn't have been too "bad" or it would have won a race by now. But I could tell Rudy thought a lot of his daddy. He must miss him a lot.

"Maybe your daddy will win next weekend."

"He promised he'd give me the trophy! Then I'm gonna have my picture taken with him and Mud Hog. And then we'll go to Tastee Freez." Rudy zoomed the race car back to its spot in the row.

He didn't seem to realize that he lived here now and wouldn't see his daddy next weekend, even if Chuck did manage to win a race by some miracle. Virginia is a long way from Alabama.

"See my comic?" Rudy flipped open a tablet and showed me a smudgy pencil story with pictures. "I'm gonna be a comic drawer when I grow up."

"I thought you were gonna be a race car driver."

"I can do both," he said, tossing the tablet on my side of our enormous room.

"Supper's ready!" Lynette called.

Doublewide quit washing in mid-lick and bounded off the bed like a kangaroo. For his size, he sure could move quick. He skidded into the kitchen, then jumped up on the extra dinette chair, waiting for his meal just like a person.

"No animals at the table," Lynette told Rudy as she set plates down.

"Doublewide is part of the family," Rudy said. "Rebel's here. *She's* family."

"Rebel is not a cat." Lynette put my plate in front of me and shooed the cat. Doublewide didn't twitch a whisker.

I stared at my plate. Shriveled pieces of meat were drowned in bright red sauce over mushy noodles. "What is this?"

"Hot dog spaghetti," Lynette said, passing around a saucer of soft white bread smeared with margarine. "Rudy's favorite. Don't you like spaghetti?"

"Regular spaghetti, yeah." I poked at a little green thing with my fork.

"Canned peas," Lynette said. "Stop picking at your food."

I finally took a bite. It tasted better than it looked, though it was kind of sweet.

Rudy speared a pea on his fork. "There's a guy on the next street with a big ol' bump on his neck like a football. I seen him. I bet he has to eat like this." He wrenched his head sideways and opened his mouth wide as a bullfrog's.

"Rudy, don't tell stories," Lynette said.

"It's not a story! I seen him with my own two eyes. He had a scarf on, but you can still see the bump. The lady next door to him won the jackpot at bingo last Friday. Three hundred dollars and a real silver pickle dish."

"You sure know a lot about people, considering you've only been here two days," I said.

"Rudy, you haven't been pestering the neighbors, have you?" my sister asked.

He shook his head. "Uh-uh. I heard about that man from—somebody. I went over to see him, is all."

I wondered who this mysterious somebody was.

"And don't go gossiping about the neighbors," Lynette warned him. "People will have a bad impression of us."

After supper, she gave Rudy two Oreos and sent him outside to play. Then we tackled the dishes.

"Rebel, I didn't tell you everything about my little boy." Lynette squirted Ivory soap into the running tap. A fine stream of bubbles floated upward. One popped on my arm, leaving a damp circle.

"Like what?" A lump of dread rose in my throat. Was Rudy a pint-sized ax murderer?

"He's crazy about his daddy, but Chuck is hardly ever around. Chuck doesn't mean to hurt Rudy's feelings, but that's just the way he is." She rinsed a yellow monster truck cup and plopped it in the drainer. "So Rudy got more—delicate-like, I guess you could say. He sleepwalks."

"He walks in his sleep?" I'd heard of people sleep-walking but never knew anyone who did. "What if he walks in his sleep tonight? What'll I do?"

"He doesn't do it every night. Only once in a while. And if he does, just lead him back to bed, easy. You don't want to wake him up."

"Will he look like he's awake?"

Lynette nodded. "He'll talk and everything. But he's really asleep. That's not all." She took a deep breath. "He has lunch with God."

I dropped the frying pan I was drying. It hit the floor with a clatter. "Do I set three places at the table?"

"Don't act smart. Hand me that skillet so I can wash it again. When it's nice out, Rudy eats his lunch on the porch steps. And, well . . . he talks to God."

"About what?" I wiped a glass calmly but my stomach quivered.

"Sometimes stuff he's worried about. Sometimes just about the weather."

The weather. My nephew discussed the weather with

God. I wondered if Rudy ever asked Him to make it snow so he could get a day off from school.

"What do you want me to do?" I asked.

"It might be a phase. Just don't make a big deal out of it, okay?"

Well, at least now I wouldn't have to worry about what I'd say to a seven-year-old all summer. Apparently God would take up the conversational slack.

Lynette had to get up early for her first day at Dot's Pink Palace Beauty Academy. She put Rudy in the tub while she redid her nails. I leafed through my *How and Why Wonder Book of Prehistoric Mammals*, but I was so tired, I kept reading the same sentence over and over.

Rudy came out of the bathroom in checkered-flag underpants, damp-haired and smelling of Prell. When he saw me, he screeched and ran into his room.

"Don't peek! I'm in my birthday suit!"

"Not quite. Put your pj's on and hop in bed, Popkin," Lynette called after him, waving her hands to dry her nails. "Don't forget your cuddly."

At last Rudy was in bed, wearing NASCAR pajamas and clasping a plastic truck that didn't look very cuddly to me.

Lynette kissed him fifty times and pulled the covers up to his chin even though it was a hundred and ten degrees. "Nighty-night, Sugar Pie. Don't let the bedbugs bite. See you in the morning, Rebel."

29

"Yeah." I had already changed the bandages on my heels and slipped into my sleep shirt. Lynette cut the light as I slid between the sheets.

And sank into a deep trough.

The bed was a canoe. I couldn't roll out of the hole!

"Rebel?" Rudy said from across the room (only a few inches away). "Will you keep that bully away from me?"

"What bully?" How come Lynette didn't tell me about *that*?

"The one next door. I'm scared to go near their house."

"Don't worry. I'll take care of any bully." It was probably some boy a year or so older than Rudy. I'd fix his little red wagon pretty fast.

"Rebel?"

"Yeah?"

"Will you let me sleep with your elephant sometimes?"

"Tusky? He's not an elephant. He's a woolly mammoth. . . . That's a kind of elephant that lived thousands of years ago." I could hear Rudy waiting for my answer. "I guess so. Sometimes."

"Tomorrow?"

"Maybe." I hoped he would drop off, so I kept quiet.

Within a few minutes, Rudy's breathing grew even. I lay awake and sweat. It was like trying to sleep in a bread box. I wondered what to do with a funeral-outfit-shopping, sleepwalking, lunch-with-God-sharing seven-year-old all day, every day, for eight weeks. Then I fell asleep too.

* * *

"Ohhh, the night they drove Old Dixie doownnn . . ."

I sat up in the dark. What the *heck* was that eerie sound?

". . . and all the people were singing . . ."

It was Rudy, singing "The Night They Drove Old Dixie Down" in a high-pitched, quavery voice. He was asleep! The notes were off-key, but he got all the words right.

This was too much. I decided to go to the bathroom. Maybe Rudy's solo would be finished by the time I got back. I heaved myself out of the canoe-bed and inched toward the door.

"Ow!" Naturally I cracked my shin on the stupid dresser. Then I made my way through the trailer without turning any lights on so I wouldn't wake Lynette.

I started to sit down on the toilet. My bare skin met something furry.

"Aiiiieee!" I stumbled backward, windmilling my arms to keep my balance.

There was a *splash!* then something large and soaking wet shot out of the toilet like a geyser. The dark shape streaked toward the door, drenching my legs and sleep shirt.

Doublewide, the Wonder Cat.

First thing tomorrow, I planned to buy a calendar so I could mark off every day I was stuck in this joint. Just like a convict.

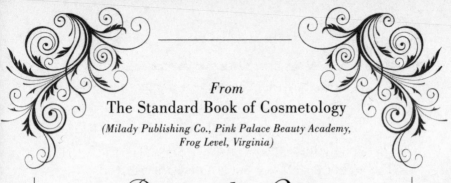

From
The Standard Book of Cosmetology
*(Milady Publishing Co., Pink Palace Beauty Academy,
Frog Level, Virginia)*

❧ *Personality Quiz* ❧

Answer One: (a) Always, (b) Sometimes, (c) Never

1. *Do* you give careful attention to personal grooming such as clothes, hair, makeup, hose, and shoes?

2. *Do* you check your posture sitting, standing, and walking erect?

3. *Do* you change undergarments regularly and avoid halitosis and body odors (B.O.) at all times?

4. *Are* you loyal to others?

5. *Are* you friendly and courteous to others?

6. *Are* you truthful in dealing with others?

7. *C*an you get along and work with others?

8. *C*an you accept responsibility?

9. *D*o you have confidence in your knowledge and ability?

10. *D*o you have a good tone of voice and choice of words?

Rating Your Personality

Give yourself 10 points for **Always**; 5 points for **Sometimes**; and zero (0) for **Never**. Compare your rating to the following standards:

Excellent Personality .85–100
Good Personality 75–80
Fair Personality. 60–70
Poor Personality . . . . .55 or less

THREE

The Bully Wore Ankle Socks

Bleary-eyed, I shook Cheerios into a bowl. I desperately needed a shower to wash off the toilet water Doublewide had splashed all over me. I tried not to worry if the cat had peed *before* I sat on him.

Lynette spent an hour in the bathroom getting ready for her first day of beauty school. She emerged with her blond hair swept to one side and enough blue eye shadow to chalk a mile-long hopscotch grid.

"See you this evening," she said. "Let Rudy sleep in. He's a growing boy. And don't forget to feed Doublewide."

"I did feed him. He's pretending I didn't," I said, glaring at the cat, who was staring forlornly into his empty dish.

"It's gonna be a great day!" Lynette said. "I already took the personality quiz in my textbook, and I got a hundred!" Then she breezed out the door with her new pink smock and the seriously dull-looking *Standard Book of Cosmetology* tucked in her black patent leather tote bag. If she had had any more personality, the world wouldn't be able to stand it.

She left before I could bring up the fact that Rudy not only walked in his sleep but performed in his sleep too. Maybe she knew, and had decided to let me discover some of his other little habits on my own.

"Rudy!" I hollered. "Breakfast!" If I couldn't sleep, he wasn't going to loll in bed all morning, growing boy or not.

A few minutes later, Rudy appeared, dragging his plastic truck. Doublewide ran over to him, casting wary glances at me. The cat's fur was still wet in patches that went the wrong way, like cowlicks.

"Here," I said, setting the bowl and a carton of milk in front of Rudy.

He pushed the bowl away. "I hate cereal."

"How can you hate cereal? It's un-American."

He went over to the refrigerator and took out an RC Cola. "Fix me a RC float. Two ice cubes and one scoop of ba-nilla ice cream. And you have to use the blue monster truck glass."

Lynette had warned me this was his standard breakfast. The soda fizzed as I poured it over ice cubes and plopped in a scoop of ice cream.

"You could *try* cereal," I said, eating the Cheerios myself. "You might like it."

"No." Foam from his float left a brownish mustache above his lip. He finished his drink with a healthy belch.

"Not bad," I said. "For a kid."

"Daddy is the best burper, but Mama always gets mad."

Little did my nephew know he stood in the presence of a champion burp-talker. I'd have shown him, but I was afraid he'd be struck down with awe. Better let him get used to my dazzling talents a bit at a time.

"Okay," I said. "Go out and play."

Rudy hesitated by the front door. "I don't wanna go by myself. Ain't you coming, too?"

"In a few minutes. I have to wash these dishes and make our beds. Now, go on."

After Rudy slunk outside, I whipped the bedspreads over rumpled sheets, then rinsed the dishes under a luke-warm tap. Good enough. Next I raced into the bathroom to take my shower.

Doublewide was using the facilities. I hadn't seen him do his business in daylight, so I leaned against the door-jamb to watch.

His hind legs splayed on the rim of the toilet seat as he leaned forward on his front feet. His tail was raised like a pump handle. He gazed straight ahead and seemed to be concentrating very hard. Then he finished and hopped down. I was disappointed he didn't flush.

Finally I had the bathroom to myself. Water trickled from Lynette's showerhead and I had to dance around to get wet. Then I changed the bandages on my heels and went outdoors.

The sky was white with heat and it wasn't even nine o'clock. Another searing day. Yippee.

I sat on the bottom porch step to practice listening. Even if I had to spend my summer Up the Creek, so to speak, I needed to keep my talents sharp.

Last year a man came to our school to give us hearing tests. He ran a big machine, and I signaled every time I heard something through the earphones. Sometimes the sounds were so faint I wasn't sure I heard them, but I signaled anyway.

Finally the man looked at his assistant and said, "There's no way she can be cheating. She can't see me adjust the dials." Then he turned to me and said, "You have extraordinary hearing, young lady. You hear almost as well as a dog!"

Since then I've been training my superhuman ability by figuring out sounds and where they are coming from.

Chip, chip, chip. That was easy. Someone was using hedge clippers two trailers down. I listened harder. *Fwoooooooosh.* That was somebody spraying a garden hose over on the next street. I blocked those sounds and closed my eyes.

Ulp. Ulp. That was a weird sound, like a guppy being strangled. It came from the direction of the backyard. I walked around the side of the trailer.

Rudy lay flat on his back in the brown grass. A scrawny

girl with limp red hair had pinned his shoulders down. Her bony elbows poked up like chicken wings. She wore a pink shorts outfit and ruffled pink ankle socks with white sandals. A long string of drool swung from her mouth directly over Rudy's face.

She sucked the drool back up with a slurp and said, "What'd I tell you about looking at me?"

"Not . . . to," Rudy said weakly.

"Are you gonna do it again?"

"No."

"No, *what*?"

"NoLaceyJaneBossoftheWorldandGrandviewEstates," he gasped.

But the girl let the drool slide back over her lip. Rudy thrashed from side to side. Then I remembered Rudy telling me about the bully next door.

This was the famous bully? This chicken-winged girl named Lacey Jane? What kind of a name was that for a bully?

I marched over and jerked the girl up by the scruff of her pink top. The drool string snapped, landing in Rudy's hair.

"Ewww!" he cried, rubbing his T-shirt over his hair.

"Hey!" the girl said, wiping spit off her chin.

"That's my nephew you're sitting on," I told her.

"Earwax? I was just teaching the little twerp who's boss."

I gave her The Look—one eye squinty, the other

drilling through the back of her head—an expression of my mother's I'd perfected. "First of all, *I'm* boss. Second of all, his name is Rudy. And third of all, if you lay a fingernail on him ever again, I'll kick your butt into next Christmas."

"Yeah? You and what army?" the girl sneered. I noticed the plastic barrettes in her skimpy hair matched her ankle socks.

I moved closer. "When I'm riled I have the strength of a saber-toothed cat attacking a spring hare."

She stepped back. "Who are you?"

"Rebel McKenzie is my name. Ask me again and I'll tell you the same."

"She's my aunt!" Rudy piped up.

"You lie," Lacey Jane said. "She's too young to be anybody's aunt."

"Lynette Parsley is my sister. She's fourteen years older than me." I put my hands on my hips. "Where do you live, Miss Mouth?"

If that girl took the personality quiz in Lynette's cosmetology book, she'd flunk quicker than a skunk trying to hide in a snowbank.

"Right there!" Rudy said, pointing to a neat gray trailer with dark blue shutters, but no flower beds or birdbaths like a lot of the other trailers. A fence with a gate divided her yard from ours.

"Maybe I should tell your mother," I said, keeping my voice level with just an edge of threat. "When she finds out you've been picking on a little kid, she'll—"

Lacey Jane's face flared red from the chest up, like a thermometer. "My mother won't do anything! So just forget about it!"

"Where is your mama?" Rudy put in. "I seen your daddy last night. He came home in a white van."

"That's his work truck," said Lacey Jane. "He's the drywall man for Merchant's Construction. So you'll go to my school," she added sourly to me.

"No. I'm only staying with Lynette for the summer while she goes to beauty school." I left out the part about being Grounded for Life. "I'm in Frog Level Middle this year."

"Estate kids go to Red Onion Elementary," she said. "I'll be in sixth grade."

"I'm in second!" Rudy said eagerly. "We'll ride the same bus!"

"Don't get any idea of sitting with me, Booger Nose." More proof this girl would score at the bottom of Lynette's personality quiz.

I punched Lacey Jane's arm. "I *told* you not to call him names. You don't listen so hot. Maybe I'll tell your mother after all—"

The ligaments in her neck popped out. "Leave my mother out of it! Go away!"

"*You're* the one in *our* yard," I said. "Are you always this grouchy?"

I wondered if Rudy had started the fight by bugging

Lacey Jane. She was probably the "somebody" who had mentioned the man with the football lump and the bingo-winning lady. Maybe Rudy pestered her about them. I could see where he might get on a person's nerves.

Reaching in the pocket of my shorts, I pulled out a roll of Necco Wafers. Paleontologists work long hours in the field and need a little sumpin' sumpin' when we start feeling peckish. So I always carry hard candy. Maybe Lacey Jane had low blood.

I peeled back the wax paper. The first wafer was chocolate, my favorite flavor. Even though Mama claimed I didn't have a scrap of manners, I held the roll out to Lacey Jane first. "Want one?"

She shook her head. "I don't like the chocolate ones."

I thumbed up the next wafer, which was pink. I hated those burny mints.

"Ooh, I love the pink ones!" Of course she did. She was a living advertisement for Pepto-Bismol.

"Let's get out of the sun," I said.

Lacey Jane lurched across the yard like she didn't have any knees.

"Do you always walk like that?" I asked.

"Like what?"

We found a speck of shade and sat down. I divided the Neccos—chocolate, green, and yellow ones for me. Lacey Jane took all the pink, purple, and orange ones. That left Rudy with the white and black ones nobody wanted.

"So what d'you like to do?" I asked Lacey Jane.

She shrugged. "Not much."

I'd known lots of kids like her. They bop along through life with no ambition. I decided to tell Lacey Jane all about myself. She *was* gobbling my candy.

"Well, I'm practically a paleontologist," I began. "I was supposed to go on a Kids' Dig in Saltville this summer, but . . . I ran into financial difficulties."

"You want to be a *what*?"

"A person who digs dead things up," Rudy broke in. He stacked his Neccos, alternating licorice and peppermint.

Lacey Jane flicked the back of his head. "Who asked you, Peanut Head?"

"Leave him alone." What was *with* this girl? One minute she was nice, the next she was the Bride of Frankenstein. "*Any*way, at school they wanted me to play softball or basketball, but I told the coach I don't like team sports. I wanted to learn fencing, but they don't teach it. Too bad, because it's a very noble sport."

Lacey Jane and even Rudy were quiet as I barreled on. Who put a nickel in me today? I always talked too much when I was nervous. Or fibbing.

"In band, I told the music teacher I didn't want to play the clarinet because there were already about a hundred clarinet players. So I picked the euphonium. There's only *one* euphonium." I leaned back in the grass. "Ainsley Carter— she's my best friend—we never hang around anybody else because they're too boring and ordinary. Ainsley wears a black beret, even in the summertime, because she believes she was a beatnik in a former life."

"What's a beatnik?" asked Rudy.

"Like a hippie, only cleaner. Ainsley plans to open a bookstore that sells only old mystery books. But she's at her grandmother's in Tennessee all summer, and now I'm stuck here—" I stopped.

Lacey Jane drew down one corner of her mouth. "Stuck in boring, ordinary Grandview Estates, you mean. With boring, ordinary people like me."

"I didn't say—" I was saved by a car whirling into the driveway of the trailer across the street.

A woman got out of the driver's side. The front of her short hair dipped in three waves. One wave was platinum blond, the middle was reddish brown, and the last wave (and the rest of her hair) was dark brown. She looked like a triple-twist Tastee Freez cone.

The woman's high heels clicked on the pavement as she walked around to the passenger door. She opened it like she was a chauffeur and the person inside was a foreign dignitary.

Out stepped a girl the same age as Lacey Jane and me. She had a plastic, blue-eyed prettiness, like those dolls you keep on a shelf. Her hair was all one color, blond, long, and curly. The sequins on her poufy yellow party dress sparkled like stars.

And—I kid you not—she wore a *tiara*. On a Monday morning!

The woman unlocked the front door of their trailer. "C'mon and rest now, sweetie."

"I want to practice my song again," the girl said. "I was a little off today."

"Don't stay in the sun long," her mother said. "You have to be careful of your fair complexion."

"I know. A young lady can never start taking care of her skin too soon." When her mother closed the door, the girl took a little bitty guitar from the front seat. Not a toy guitar—just small.

Then she planted her yellow strap shoes wide apart and began strumming the little guitar.

"Yessir, that's my baby. Nossir, don't mean maybe—" As she played and sang, she wiggled her hips in time.

Suddenly the girl arched backward like she was having a fit and swung the little guitar over her head. With her arms bent at a weird angle, she strummed the guitar *behind her head* and kept singing.

"That's my baby noooooooow!"

My jaw dropped in astonishment. "What *is* that?" I asked.

"That," Lacey Jane replied dryly, "is Bambi Lovering. Just one of the ordinary, boring people in Grandview Estates."

From the Field Notebook
of Rebel McKenzie

When people think about Ice Age animals—
and they don't think about them *nearly*
enough—they always mention the saber-
toothed lion.

Its real name is *Smilodon*. You say it
SMILE-o-don. These cats weighed almost
900 pounds and had powerful muscles in their
shoulders so they could knock down their prey.
Their paws were as big as turkey platters.
And they had long curved canine teeth called
sabers. The sabers were eight inches long!

Scientists used to think that *Smilodon*
jumped on its prey and ripped its throat
open. Blood would gush everywhere, and the

animal would bleed to death, if it didn't die of shock first at seeing those great big long front teeth.

But paleontologists, who are way smarter than regular scientists, studied the fossil teeth of Smilodon. The saber teeth never had any marks on them like from nicking neck bones. They figured out that the big cats tore into the soft underbellies of their prey instead.

Sneaky, huh?

FOUR

Bambi Lovering's Expert Beauty Tips

Bambi's nose practically touched the ground as she ended her performance with a deep curtsy. I'd never seen anyone curtsy except in the movies, and never that low. I wondered how she kept from toppling over.

Rudy clapped enthusiastically. I nudged his arm. "Quit it."

But Bambi spotted us and trotted across the street, yellow skirts billowing. She waved like she was riding on a parade float.

"Hi!" she chirped. "Y'all just move in?"

"My sister did," I said. "I'm just staying for the summer to take care of Rudy here while she goes to beauty school. I'm Rebel."

"Hi, Rebel! Hi, Rudy!"

Rudy gaped at Bambi like a catfish till I elbowed him

again. He closed his mouth but didn't take his eyes off her.

"I guess you already know Lacey Jane," I said, since Lacey Jane just stood there with her lips pressed tight.

"Mmm." Bambi tipped her head back as if she smelled something unpleasant. Then she flashed a practiced smile. "What'd you think of my song? The judges gave me first place in talent."

"But last place in modesty," Lacey Jane finally spoke.

"Were you in a contest or something?" I asked.

"The John Deere Culpeper dealership beauty pageant. Young Miss category," Bambi replied expansively. "I placed first in talent and overall appearance, naturally. But only second in personality because a bumblebee flew up my skirt while I was telling the judges my life's ambition."

"Poor bee probably died from the stink."

I giggled at Lacey Jane's remark.

"Did you get stung?" Rudy asked Bambi, all concerned.

She pursed her lips in a pout. "No, but I got distracted, which is even worse. You shouldn't let anything bother you during the judges' interview. They took off points and I came in second."

"So you lost," Lacey Jane said gleefully.

"I can tell you two are best friends," I said, looking from one to the other. Lacey Jane clearly couldn't stand Bambi; but then, Lacey Jane didn't much like anybody from what I'd seen.

"Hardly." Lacey Jane gave a wicked grin. "Poor little beauty queen didn't win the crown."

"I'll have you know, second place was a tiara, a check for five hundred dollars, and an official John Deere T-shirt and ball cap," Bambi said smugly. "I gave Daddy the John Deere stuff. Mama will probably put the check in the bank. I have my own savings account with all the money I've earned from beauty pageants."

I slapped my forehead, staggering. "Five hundred *dollars*? And all you did was play that little guitar and sing that weird song?"

"It's a ukulele. A Hawaiian guitar." She held up the four-string guitar by the neck. "The other girls jump around the stage in satin shorts and do stuff like the splits. Me, I come out and sing and pluck my ukulele. The judges think I'm charming."

"You played it behind your *head*," I said.

Bambi grinned. "Neat, huh? I made that part up myself. Mama says it adds sparkle to my act."

Lacey Jane strummed an imaginary guitar and sang mockingly, "That's my baby noooooooooow!"

Bambi's brows drew together. Suddenly she wasn't so pretty. "You're just jealous, Lacey Jane Whistle, because I'm going to make something of myself!"

That snagged my attention. Bambi didn't seem like the type who had goals in life. "What do you want to do?" I asked.

"First, I'll win the Miss Virginia pageant. Then I'll be crowned Miss America—"

Lacey Jane pretended to throw up. "Yeah, right!"

Bambi ignored her. "Miss America gets a big scholarship. I'm going to business college, and when I get out I'm going to be a beauty expert and have my own beauty empire—products, an advice column, maybe even a TV show."

Well, if that didn't beat all. I guess with a name like Bambi Lovering, I shouldn't expect her to aim to cure cancer.

"I've already started on my life's plan," she rattled on. "I have my own column in our school newspaper. It's called 'Bambi Lovering's Expert Beauty Tips.' My teacher said sales of *Red Onion Peels* doubled once my column started in it."

"I'm surprised you haven't been sued yet," said Lacey Jane. "You name names in that stupid column!"

"How was I to know Kady Blackwell would shave the hair off her arms with her daddy's razor?" Bambi said loftily. "I just *mentioned* that if she didn't want to set her arm hair on rollers, she might try a bleach cream, is all."

Rudy gawked at Bambi like she was made out of cake. "Will you come over and play with me sometime?"

She glanced at him. "I'm awful busy with singing lessons and the beauty advice book I'm writing." Then she fastened her round doll's eyes on me. "You could do with a little work, Rebel. You don't make the most of what you have."

"And what would that be?" I asked, even though I didn't give a fig about my looks.

She walked all around me like I was a car in a show-room, tapping her index finger on her chin. "Hmmm. Your eyelashes are on the puny side, but your hair is nice and thick. You should curl it instead of letting it hang there like a raggy curtain."

"My hair is fine the way it is."

Bambi let out a tragic sigh. "Too bad. You don't have *one* single natural sign of beauty."

Lacey Jane rolled her eyes skyward. "Here we go. Another episode of why Bambi Lovering is the star of the universe and everybody else is ugly as a mud fence."

"I possess three natural signs of beauty," Bambi began, like she was telling a fairy tale. She pulled her bangs back. "See that vee? That's a widow's peak. Most people have plain old hairlines, like yours. I also have large front teeth—"

"Beaver teeth," Lacey Jane remarked. I snickered. When Lacey Jane wasn't being a bully, she was a real cutup.

Bambi glared at her. "I do *not* have beaver teeth! Mama says my teeth are pretty as wedding china and I could be a toothpaste model. My final sign of beauty is this mole under my left eye." She pointed to a tiny dark spot I thought was an ink mark. "Back in the days of George

Washington, ladies used to paste fake moles on their face. Sometimes the moles were shaped like hearts or moons or stars. Mama told me all this because on the day I was born—"

"The worst day in the history of the world," Lacey Jane said.

"—the nurse laid me in my mama's arms and said, 'Mrs. Lovering, that child is a natural beauty.' Since then Mama's been studying up on natural beauties like Marilyn Monroe and Scarlett O'Hara and Elizabeth Taylor. I wish I had violet eyes like Elizabeth Taylor, but I do have a ring around my iris. See it?"

A yawn pushed out of my mouth that I didn't bother to hide. "Do you *ever* talk about anything but yourself?" I talked about *my*self, but at least I was interesting.

She peered at me. "Is that a ring around your iris? No. Well, you *almost* had a natural sign of beauty."

"Bambi," said Lacey Jane. "Shut up."

"You shut up. You're still mad about the last day of school." Bambi explained to me, "Leonard Smoot pushed her down when we got off the bus and later he took me to the movies. Lacey Jane had a big crush on him all year."

Lacey Jane balled her fists. "I did not! You think every boy alive is madly in love with you!"

"I love you," said Rudy in a small voice. Naked infatuation lit his pale face.

Oh, brother. I wondered if Rudy would sleepwalk over

to Bambi's trailer and serenade her with "The Night They Drove Old Dixie Down."

Bambi patted his cheek. "Bless your pea-picking little heart!" All business again, she announced, "This summer I'm doing a special back-to-school package. Head-to-toe makeover for only five dollars. Plus two typed pages of beauty hints, and that *includes* your colors! What do you say?"

"I say, buzz off." Where did that girl get her nerve?

"You're missing a fabulous opportunity."

Across the street, the front door of her trailer opened, and her mother called out, "C'mon in, sugar. I drew a nice cool oatmeal bath for you." The door closed again.

"Think it over," Bambi said, heading home. "Especially you, Lacey Jane. With looks like yours, you don't have a minute to lose—"

Before I could blink, Lacey Jane flew at Bambi, clawing the tiara off her head.

"Oww!" Bambi cried. The tiara was tangled in her curls, but Lacey Jane kept yanking.

I grabbed her arm. "Let's get out of here before her mother comes after us!"

"Go soak your stupid head in your stupid oatmeal bath!" Lacey Jane yelled over her shoulder as I dragged her away.

"Redheads should never wear pink!" Bambi fired back. "You look pukeish!"

I tugged Lacey Jane down the street toward the firehouse. Rudy reluctantly tripped along behind us, already pining for his True Love.

"Did you and Bambi have words before you fell out?" I asked Lacey Jane.

The skin under her eyes grew tight. "I don't want to talk about it, okay?"

"Okay, okay." Lacey Jane was like a live bomb. You never knew what would set off her (very short) fuse.

At the station, two firemen hosed a big red truck parked on the cement driveway. Rudy ran up to one of them and blurted, "Hey, did you just come from a fire? Did the house burn down? Did anybody die?"

I expected him to whip out his fashion magazines and offer to pick out the victim's funeral outfits.

"Rudy Parsley," I bellowed. "Get over here."

Inside the firehouse the break room was cool and dim. Cracked plastic chairs faced a battered TV set. A bank of vending machines lined one wall.

"What do you want?" Lacey Jane asked, standing in front of the soda machine.

"I don't have any money." I still had my ten bucks, but I owed Skeeter twenty, and I didn't know when he'd be sprung from prison.

"Daddy leaves me a few dollars before he goes to work." Lacey Jane fed a bill into the machine. "Dr Pepper okay?" She punched the button, and the bottle rolled down.

I popped the cap while she debated over the snack selections. "We need salt to get rid of the sugar taste from all those Neccos we ate."

"You mean all that sickening sweetness from Bambi." Lacey Jane pulled the knob for a bag of barbecue potato chips.

"Me first!" Rudy said, reaching for the Dr Pepper.

"You last." As I sipped from the bottle, I noticed a poster bristling with exclamation points by the candy machine. "Hey, look at this."

Lacey Jane read the poster out loud. "'Announcing the Second Annual Frog Level Volunteer Firemen's Carnival. Games, Prizes, Rides Galore! Beauty Pageant! Four Age Categories! Two Hundred Fifty Dollars Top Prize!'"

"A beauty pageant," I breathed. And *prize* money. A pot of gold to finance my trip to the August Kids' Dig. "Let's enter!"

Lacey Jane stared at me. "Us? Enter a beauty pageant? Are you crazy?"

"Why not? We're not homely." Actually, Lacey Jane was, a little. Okay, more than a little. But her face wouldn't make a train jump the tracks or anything. "I think it'll be fun. Let's do it."

"Did you read the fine print?" Her finger stabbed a line at the bottom of the poster.

$25 APPLICATION FEE. REGISTER AT BETTER-OFF-DEAD PEST CONTROL AND BRIDAL CONSIGNMENT.

"Dang." My pot-of-gold bubble burst. "I'm broker than four o'clock."

"My dad will lend you the money if you need it," Lacey Jane offered.

"I couldn't take your father's money." But if I won, I could pay him back. And Skeeter. *And* have enough left over to go to Saltville. I could almost taste the Bison Bacon. But would her father be so keen to lend me money if Lacey Jane wasn't in the contest, too? "I'm not entering unless you do," I said.

"What about Bambi? She's a twit, but she's still pretty stiff competition."

"Did she enter last year?"

The skin tightened under Lacey Jane's eyes again. "I don't know. We didn't go to the firemen's carnival last summer."

"I bet she won't even bother with this piddly little contest," I said. "Anyway, we look just as good as her."

Lacey Jane twisted a piece of her lank hair. "I don't have curly hair like Bambi."

"So? My sister will fix your hair. She's practically a licensed beautician."

She kept throwing boulders in the road. "We don't have any talent."

"Who says we don't?" I protested. "You're loaded with talent. I bet you can't walk across the floor without twirling two hula hoops and yodeling."

"Well . . . maybe." She cracked a smile. "How about you? What's your talent?"

"Yeah," Rudy said. "What's your talent, Rebel?"

"I'll show you."

Holding my breath, I gulped three big swigs of Dr Pepper. Gas rumbled in my stomach. I opened my mouth to release a giant belch. But instead of just letting it rip, I formed my lips into words.

"ConnecticutMassachusettsVirginiaSouthCarolinaNorth CarolinaGeorgiaNewHampshireNewJerseyNewYorkMaryland DelawarePennsylvaniaaaaaaaaaa . . ."

As always, I petered out on "Pennsylvania."

Lacey Jane and Rudy stared at me, goggle-eyed. "You just burped the thirteen colonies," said Lacey Jane, astonished.

"Except for Rhode Island. I can't ever get the thirteenth colony out."

Lacey Jane cracked up. She slid down the wall and plunked spraddle-legged on the floor, snorting Dr Pepper out of her nose. Rudy started giggling, and I did too as I collapsed beside Lacey Jane.

Our laughter echoed all over the firehouse. Rudy and me, our laughs sounded regular, like everybody else's. But Lacey Jane's laugh sounded like music rippling from an old piano that hadn't been played for a long time.

❀*Bambi Lovering's*
EXPERT BEAUTY TIPS
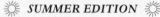
☀ *SUMMER EDITION* ☀

---

*W*hat do you do if you have "piano legs" like Lacey Jane Whistle? Don't wear short shorts! People can see your legs are the same size all the way down!

If you don't want to be mistaken for a stool or something, wear Bermuda shorts. They hit at the knee and people will think you just have shapeless calves. Never *ever* wear babyish ankle socks, especially with sandals! This is a fashion "faux pas" you see all over the magazines.

Also, if you're a redhead like Lacey Jane Whistle, you can't get a tan. All you do is burn and peel, even if you slap on a gallon of Caribbean Pete Banana Coconut Oil. Don't show your snow-white piano legs in short shorts. Not unless you give the rest of us sunglasses so we don't go blind.

Finally, never wear *pink* short shorts if you are a redhead with piano legs. That breaks so many fashion rules I can't count them all.

Until next time . . . smile pretty!

*B*ambi Lovering,
Your Expert Beauty Consultant

Rudy and Rebul at the Truck Rac

Are we gon to win today?

I don no. I hop so.

Let me hav sum of that.

Rebul gets a humbuger and friz.

Look heer they com! Com on Mud Hog!

The trucks are nec and nec.

Hurry up and win!

Rebul gets up.

Then she falls don.

My stomick hurts.

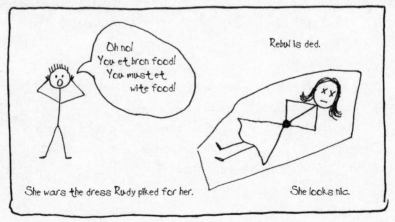

Oh no! You et bron food! You must et wite food!

Rebul is ded.

She wars the dress Rudy piked for her.

She looks nic.

FIVE

Better-Off-Dead Pest Control and Bridal Consignment

At six fifteen, Lynette stumbled in the door. The front of her pink smock was streaked with dye, her makeup was smudged, and her hair stuck out everywhere. She looked like she'd sailed around the world in a teacup.

She tossed her textbook on the kitchen floor and burst into tears.

"What?" I hurried over to her. "Did you wreck The Clunker?"

"I'm a dumb bunny in school! And the old biddies at the beauty parlor h-h-hate meeee!" she wailed, falling into a heap on her Spanish modern sofa.

Rudy hopped up from the puzzle he was putting together on the rug and laid his small palm on her back. "You're not a dumb bunny, Mama."

"Yes, I am! I can't even say circalutory—circa—cir—"

"Circulatory?" I provided.

"Yes! I couldn't say that word and Miss Dot's lips got all thin. I bet she fails me! And on my first day at Hair Magic, one lady complained to Virina—she's the owner—that I scratched her scalp when I shampooed her color out. She wanted her money back!" She broke into a fresh wave of sobs.

"What do you care about circulatory stuff?" I asked. "You're not going to air-conditioning school."

Lynette sat up. "Oh, Rebel, you have no idea. We have to learn all about skin diseases like acne and eczema and scabies. We have to learn *chemistry* and *hygiene* and *anatomy* and the *digestive* system, and circalu—that word!"

"Circulatory system. You have to know about blood and guts to fix hair?"

Lynette blew her nose on her smock. "If I make it—*if*—I'll be a hairdresser *and* a doctor."

"Really?" Rudy's eyes grew wide.

"No. But I might as well, all the stuff they make us study." She grabbed my hand like a drowning person grasping a rope. "You'll help me, won't you, Rebel?"

"I said I would yesterday." I pulled her up. "Go wash your face. Supper's almost ready."

After Lynette scuffed into the bathroom, I wrapped a tea towel around my hand and took three TV dinners out of the oven. A nice, hot meal would make my sister feel better. Rudy had already set the table—paper towels

61

folded in triangles for napkins, knives and forks precisely lined up beside the plates. And everyone got a different monster truck cup.

Lynette trudged into the kitchen, her face scrubbed and her hair skinned back in a ponytail. She sat down, tying the belt of her pink chenille robe. "What's this?"

"Macaroni and cheese with peas and Apple Delight," I replied brightly. "Delicioso."

Rudy covered his plate with his napkin. "I don't like cheese on macaroni."

"*Every*body likes macaroni and cheese," I said, the chipperness in my tone slipping a notch.

"Rebel, I bought the TV dinners for me and you," Lynette said. "I told you Rudy only eats hot dog spaghetti for lunch and dinner. Didn't you hear me?"

I flung my fork down. "You also told me to get him to eat other stuff!"

"I don't want any supper," Rudy declared.

Dropping her face in her hands, Lynette began crying again. "My little baby is starving! I can't be here to cook for him because I have to go to school and be the dumbest one in class!"

"Rudy is *not* starving," I said sternly. "He had an RC float for breakfast like always. Then he had a bunch of Necco Wafers, part of a Dr Pepper, and some barbecue potato chips. And that revolting spaghetti crap for lunch."

I didn't tell Lynette I'd scorched the hot dogs and the noodles were undercooked, but Rudy dutifully took his plate out on the steps. I couldn't see anybody, but I could hear Rudy talking, so I guess God showed up for his usual lunch date.

Rudy's lips were tucked in like a buttonhole. I snatched his plate and marched over to the sink. Scraping the macaroni and cheese in a strainer, I held it under the running faucet. When every smidge of cheese had been rinsed off, I dumped worm-white macaroni on Rudy's plate and stomped back over to the table.

"Here, Your Highness," I said. "Macaroni with *no* cheese. Shall I peel your peas and vacuum the apples out of the crust?"

His chin quivered.

"Don't you start bawling too," I said, then added, "Eat your supper and I'll teach you to burp-talk."

"Oh, boy!" He wolfed the cold macaroni like it was pheasant under glass.

Lynette stood up. "I'm not really hungry, Rebel. I need to read two chapters in my book tonight."

"I slave over hot TV dinners and this is the thanks I get?" I waved her away. "It's okay. I don't mind cleaning up."

I washed the dishes while Lynette mumbled over her textbook and Rudy worked on his puzzle. Worn to a nubbin from my own tough day, I turned the TV on to a science program about carpenter ants. Perfect. I flopped in one of the ugly black chairs.

Doublewide jumped up on top of the TV, hunkered down so his paws draped over the screen, and stared at me.

"You have food in your dish," I told the cat. "Now, move so I can see."

"It's time for his favorite show," Rudy said, trying to cram a corner piece in the center of the border.

"The *cat* has a favorite TV show?"

"Reruns of *Wagon Train*." Lynette thumbed through her book. "He thinks the horse teams are mice. Put it on channel thirty-three."

I crossed my arms over my chest. "I am *not* changing channels for a cat. Scram!"

Doublewide crossed his eyes and didn't budge.

"Oh, no," Lynette moaned. "Miss Dot assigned *eighty-five* pages in this horrible book. I can't do this." She broke down boohooing again.

Rudy ripped up half of his puzzle, and pieces flew across the room. "I hate this ol' puzzle!"

I was surrounded by a bunch of crankypants. But I was worried about my sister. Always the strong one, she was unraveling like the scarf I'd knitted the five minutes I'd been a Girl Scout. Instead of substituting one mother for another this summer, it seemed *I'd* become the mother.

Then I remembered what Daddy had done once when

I got frustrated because the mastodon I'd copied from my *How and Why Wonder Book of Prehistoric Mammals* looked more like King Kong.

I fetched a couple of vanilla pudding cups from the refrigerator and two spoons from the silverware drawer.

"C'mon," I said, herding Lynette toward her room. "You too, Rudy."

I settled them both in the sloshy water bed, gave Lynette her textbook, Rudy a Spider-Man comic, and each a pudding cup and spoon.

"You'll feel better in a little bit," I said, easing the door shut.

"Give one to Doublewide," Rudy called after me. "He loves pudding."

In the kitchen I took the last pudding cup for myself, then tumbled in my chair again. Alone at last.

Almost.

Doublewide still claimed the top of the TV. His blue eyes lasered into mine.

"All right, you win." I got up and switched the channel. On the screen, Ward Bond bellowed, "Wa-gons *ho*!"

Doublewide sprang off the TV and leaped up into my seat before I made it back.

"Oh, no, you don't." I tried to nudge the cat aside, but it was like shoving an anvil. We finally came to an agreement—he sprawled over most of the chair while I was scrunched in the corner.

I dipped my spoon into the creamy, smooth pudding. "Mmmm."

The cat's head whirled around so fast, I was surprised he didn't get whiplash.

"Uh-uh."

He bunched himself up, pretending to be a pitiful little kitten instead of a twenty-one-pound lard bucket.

With a sigh, I propped the cup in front of him. He lapped the pudding happily, his whiskers daintily pinned back.

I had to bust out of this loony bin. Winning the Frog Level Volunteer Fire Department's beauty pageant was my only ticket. I couldn't ask Lynette for the registration fee—she was already a basket case. Somehow I'd find the money.

That decided, I made myself comfortable in the two inches of space allotted me and watched *Wagon Train* with Doublewide.

As soon as The Clunker rolled out of the driveway the next morning, I hauled Rudy across the strip of crabgrass to Lacey Jane's trailer.

"I'm not going in there!" he yelled, clinging to the clothes pole. "That awful girl lives there!"

"We're friends now, remember?" I told him, prying his fingers off one by one.

"You can't make me!"

I prodded him up the steps of the Whistle trailer and knocked. When Lacey Jane answered, Rudy crumpled on the doorsill like a sack of potatoes.

"Rebel!" she cried. "What's wrong with the kid?"

"Nothing." Stooping, I clasped Rudy around his middle and dragged him inside. He lay on the floor limp as a ten-cent dishrag, but his eyeballs rolled under his eyelids. "Get up, you faker, or you'll eat boiled turnips for lunch."

"Are you sure he's okay?" Lacey Jane said.

"Yeah. He's a just a big mama's baby."

Rudy sat up. "I am not a baby!" Then he glanced at Lacey Jane. "I was kinda scared to come in here, but Rebel made me."

"We don't always get our way in this world," I said. Wasn't I living proof? I should have been dusting the molar of a fossilized musk-ox right about now.

Guilt flickered in Lacey Jane's eyes. Was she sorry for picking on Rudy? She thrust a pink paper under my nose. "Look what was stuck in our mailbox."

I skimmed the paper. "I can't believe Bambi sent you this!"

"I can. Where does that twerp get off giving me beauty tips!" Lacey Jane flipped a scraggly pigtail over her shoulder. "I do *not* have piano legs!"

Suddenly my job became a lot easier. "We have to get back at her. We'll enter the beauty pageant, us against Bambi Lovering."

"Why would she even enter? Yesterday you said she probably thinks our pageant is piddly."

"She'll enter, all right," I said. "She can't pass up another tiara. But you'll win instead, and Bambi will go into a decline. She'll never get over it. She'll be a hermit and nobody will ever—"

Lacey Jane stopped listening and said, "What makes you think I'll win?"

"Because . . ." I had to step careful here. "Because you're not a phony like Bambi. The judges will see that you, Lacey Jane, are the real thing."

I needed Lacey Jane to enter with me because a) her father would lend me the registration money, and b) even though I didn't have a widow's peak or a beauty mark, Lacey Jane's plainness would make me look like Cleopatra by comparison. I had enough competition with Bambi and her ukulele.

"What about you?" she said, as if reading my mind. "What if the judges think *you're* the real thing instead of me?"

"They won't," I said quickly. "I'm just entering to make you stand out even more." I relaxed my face so it would sag like an old hammock. I looked unattractive and also not too bright.

Lacey Jane studied me for a second. "Okay. Let me get my shoes on." She disappeared down the hall.

For the first time, I checked out her trailer. The living

room was slab by the kitchen, like Lynette's. An orange afghan lay balled up at one end of the blue plaid sofa.

"That's a pretty afghan," I said when Lacey Jane returned wearing blue ankle socks with her sandals. "Did your mother crochet it?"

She nodded but said nothing as she locked the front door behind us.

We walked up Grandview Lane, the main road of the trailer park. It was so hot, my flip-flops stuck to the soft asphalt.

Lacey Jane noticed my bandaged heels. "What happened to your feet?"

"Rebel runned away," Rudy piped up. "But she had on the wrong shoes."

"The next time I leave home, I'll be sure to wear special running-away shoes."

"You really ran away?" Lacey Jane glanced at me with new respect.

I told her the whole sordid story. When I was finished, Lacey Jane didn't seem that impressed. "I thought you ran off because your parents are mean," she said.

"I'm grounded till I'm fifty. If that isn't mean, I don't know what is."

Grandview Lane ended at Greycliff Road. The shopping center sat at the intersection. It consisted of the 7-Eleven, Sudz 'N Dudz Laundromat, Hair Magic (the beauty parlor where Lynette worked in the afternoons), and

Better-Off-Dead Pest Control and Bridal Consignment.

A sign in the window of the last store declared that Better-Off-Dead Pest Control and Bridal Consignment was the official sponsor of the Miss Frog Level Volunteer Fire Department Pageant.

I pushed the door open. A blast of air-conditioning almost smacked us flat. The shop was really two stores in one. Filmy white curtains hung over a doorway marked BRIDAL CONSIGNMENT.

An army of plastic termites marched across the counter of the pest control part. An old man with a floppy stomach like a shopping bag swiveled his desk chair around.

"Hey there, kids. What can I do you for?"

"We're here to sign up for the beauty pageant," said Lacey Jane.

He pointed to the curtained doorway. "In there. Mama will help you." That old man had a mother? She must be a hundred and two.

We walked into the bridal consignment part. Racks of fancy dresses lined the walls. A mannequin wearing a rhinestone-spangled wedding gown stood in the center. Clamped over the model's crooked wig was a rhinestone headband with a short veil.

Up close, I could see the dress was grubby around the hem and the veil was dusty. A tattoo of an anchor adorned the mannequin's left forearm. Someone had tried unsuccessfully to scrub it off.

All this frilly stuff made me feel choky and I began to cough. A woman not much bigger than Rudy emerged from the back. I thought she was a kid, but then I noticed her little hanging stomach. Pest Control Man's mama. She *was* ancient.

"Hello," she said, smiling through a sea of wrinkles. "I'm Mrs. Randolph. How can I help you?"

"We want to be in the beauty pageant," I said.

On the tiniest feet I'd ever seen on a grown-up, she tottered over to a desk, pulled a drawer open, and took out a clipboard and pencil.

"Names?" As Lacey Jane and I spelled our names, she wrote them down.

Reading upside-down-and-backward—another special talent of mine—I spotted Bambi Lovering's name at the top of the list. So Bambi *had* entered the pageant!

The woman handed us each an application form. "Fill this out, have a parent or guardian sign it, and bring it back to me with your entry fee."

Outside again, the heat slapped us like a scalding washcloth. Lacey Jane said, "I have two dollars. Let's get Slurpees."

"You're my friend for life!" I gushed, stepping into the cool oasis of my favorite store.

Lacey Jane gave me a funny look, but said nothing.

The 7-Eleven was empty except for the clerk and an older woman piling groceries on the counter. While she counted change from her wallet, we ordered three blueberry Slurpees. The clerk dispensed the slushy drinks into tall plastic cups.

Lacey Jane paid, then we went outside and sat on a bench. I pulled on the straw so hard, ice-pick pain jabbed my skull. Delicioso. Rudy fumbled with his straw until I stabbed it into the X cut in the lid.

Lacey Jane scanned her paper. "'Age divisions. Sweet Pea, three to five. Daisy, six to eight. Violet, nine to twelve. Rose, thirteen to fifteen.' We're Violets."

The older woman came out of the 7-Eleven with two large bags. She adjusted her grip and squinted up at the blazing sun.

"Gaggy names," I said, checking out my own form. "'Three Words That Describe You.' How about brilliant, beautiful, and—bombastic!"

Lacey Jane giggled. "For hobbies, put down burping!"

"That's great! Got a pencil?"

The woman set her bags on the concrete and mopped her shiny face with a handkerchief. She wore cotton gloves, which seemed weird. I was too hot to wear a part in my hair, much less gloves.

"I saw Bambi Lovering's name on the contest list," I said.

Lacey Jane grinned with blue-stained lips. "She doesn't stand a chance against our gorgeous selves."

"She might as well drop out!" I pretended to clink my cup against hers.

"Yeah!" Rudy echoed. He slammed his cup into ours. Blueberry slush spilled over our fingers.

"Rudy!" I swiped my sticky hand on his knee.

Lacey Jane striped Slurpee across my cheek. I flicked my straw at her, spattering her shirt with blue specks.

"The pageant judges won't look twice at Bambi," I said, giggling. "You're a cinch to win. And I'll get second place, easy."

The woman frowned at me, gloved hands on her hips. "Not till groundhogs boogie."

MISS FROG LEVEL VOLUNTEER FIRE DEPARTMENT PAGEANT

ENTRY FORM

Sponsored By
Better-Off-Dead Pest Control and Bridal Consignment
*"When you have bugs or an unused wedding dress,
think of us!"*

Age Division (check one): Sweet Pea (3–5):___
Daisy (6–8):___ Violet (9–12):_ X _ Rose (13–15):___

Name: Rebel McKenzie
Address: 8705-B Grandview Lane, Frog Level, Virginia
Phone: 555-8770

Parent/Guardian: *Lynette Parsley* (older sister,
and that's her real signature—she can't help it she
writes like a kid)

Eyes: Brown **Hair:** Brown **Grade:** going into 7th (though
I should be in college)

Three Words That Describe You: Kind, Thoughtful, (very)
Nice

Hobbies: Digging fossils up, reading my favorite book, *The How and Why Wonder Book of Prehistoric Mammals*

Ambition: to be a paleontologist (the Ice Age kind, not the dinosaur kind)

Three People You Most Admire:
1. Dr. Paul E. Blackwood, the author of *The How and Why Wonder Book of Prehistoric Mammals*, even though he is probably dead
2. My parents (okay, that's two)
3. Mr. Brawley, principal of Frog Level Elementary School

Type of Talent: too many to list!

PAGEANT RULES:

- If you are performing a musical talent, bring your own music
- Off-the-rack dresses for Appearance, sportswear for athletic Talent
- No pageant attire!
- *Judges' decisions are final*

SIX

Stealing the Deal

"What do you mean?" I asked, looking up at the woman. I didn't really want an answer, but since she was butting in, she owed us an explanation.

"Beauty pageants aren't so easy to ace," she replied. "Don't roll your eyes at me, missy. I know what I'm talking about."

"*You* were in a beauty contest?" I said in disbelief.

"I used to model. Same difference."

If my jaw hadn't been hinged to my skull, it would have dropped in my lap. Even I knew that models were pretty and skinny. This frizzy-haired old woman was built like a fire hydrant. Her pudding-plain face was studded with little raisin eyes and a blobby nose. Maybe she once modeled Halloween masks.

The woman started to heft her bags again. "Law, I do

it every time. Come up here to pick up one or two things and wind up with more than I can tote."

"We'll help." Lacey Jane leaped to her feet, tossing her Slurpee cup in the trash. "Rebel, you take this one." She gave me a bulging sack apparently filled with plutonium bricks. The other bag had a loaf of Wonder bread peeking out the top.

I was brimming with questions, but followed the woman down Greycliff Road. Who was she? And why was she wearing gloves? Was she a cat burglar? I could see her knocking over candy stores easier than I could picture her modeling dresses.

"Miz Matthews," Lacey Jane said. She sounded respectful. Not at all like her usual prickly self. "You shouldn't be walking in this heat. How come you don't drive a car?"

"I can't see like I did." She chuckled. "Viola Sandbanks would carry me to the store any time I want. But she runs on about Palmer and the mailman so, I forget what I'm going after."

"Who's Viola Sandbanks?" I asked. "Who's Palmer? And who are *you*?"

"Lands, this heat's made me overlook my manners. I'm Miss Odenia Matthews. You're the little sister of the lady who rents Mr. Shifflett's mobile home."

"*Younger* sister," I corrected. "Rebel McKenzie. What about this Palmer and the mailman?"

"You'll meet them tomorrow afternoon," said Miss Odenia. "Well, not Mr. Beechley because he has his route and wouldn't come on a bet. He's so terrified of Palmer Sandbanks, he just throws the mail in our boxes all mixed up, and I have to stand there and sort it out. I don't want anyone to think *I* receive those racy lingerie catalogs."

"Tomorrow afternoon?" I felt mixed up myself. Tar blisters rose like soup bubbles, and haze shimmered over the road like a mirage.

I don't know why Lacey Jane was so worried about the old woman walking in the heat. Miss Odenia strode ahead like Grant taking Richmond. Her white blouse was fresh-from-the-dryer crisp. Pit stains soaked my T-shirt clear to my kneecaps.

Even Rudy noticed. "You need some be-odorant. Get it? B.O.?"

"When the feeling comes back in my hands, I'm going to swat you one."

Miss Odenia frowned at me. "That's the very thing I'm talking about. If you girls are serious about this beauty pageant, you must speak politely. And you can't gallop onstage and carry on like hoydens."

Hoydens! What a funny word! I giggled.

Miss Odenia froze me with a Look scarier than the Squint-eye my mother used. Mama could take Look lessons from this old lady.

"You won't be judged just on appearance, but also

personality," she went on. "You need to be confident, not brash."

"I *am* confident," I protested. "I'm practically a paleontologist."

"Maybe," she said doubtfully, "but you sadly lack grace and poise."

"Grace? What does that thing we say on Thanksgiving got to do with the price of tea in China?" I asked.

"You know very well what I mean. Mocking is a bad habit. Along with slouching and lumping along like a camel."

She must have been talking about Lacey Jane. She lurched down the road, leaning forward like she was pushing against a hurricane.

"Miz Odenia, can you help us?" Lacey Jane said as we entered the trailer park.

She nodded. "I'd be glad to give you pageant tips."

I didn't believe she was doing this out of the puredee goodness of her heart. She had to have a reason. "How come?" I asked point-blank. "What's in it for you?"

"Rebel!" Lacey Jane said, shocked. "When somebody says they're going to help you, you don't ask them why!"

"Rebel has a right to be cautious," said Miss Odenia. "She doesn't know me from Noah's house cat. As it happens, I do want a favor in return."

"What?" I said.

We stopped in front of Miss Odenia's trailer, the one

with the ceramic kittens climbing the shutters and the flower beds and the plaster frog in the birdbath.

She clucked her tongue as we walked to the front door. "I'd better tackle those weeds in the portulaca when it cools off. C'mon in. I have lemonade in the Frigidaire."

We followed her inside. I gratefully dumped the grocery bag on the kitchen counter and shook my numb fingers to get the circulation stirring again.

"I'll bring the drinks into the living room," Miss Odenia told us.

Her living room was nothing like Lynette's. Old dark wood chairs were covered in faded flower print material. Tables displayed black-and-white photographs in silver frames. But no people, at least not whole people . . . just *hands*.

There were framed magazine advertisements of hands touching toasters, holding telephones, flaunting diamond rings. Between the frames, statues of hands wore draped bead necklaces or fancy gloves. Over the sofa hung a gigantic photograph of a hand.

Creeped out, I elbowed Lacy Jane and whispered, "Next time, warn me."

Lacey Jane's eyes were practically out on stalks. "I've never been in here before either," she whispered back. "Miz Odenia's always watched us kids when she was outside working in her yard."

I stared at a photo of a hand holding a carving knife. "What's wrong with pictures of kittens?"

"I think it's neat," Rudy said. No surprise. His taste was all in his mouth, or else why would he have a crush on Bambi?

"Here we go." Miss Odenia set a tray of glasses on the coffee table. She had taken off her gloves. I tried to see if her fingertips were sandpapered, like a safecracker's. "Now, let's get down to brass tacks. You girls are in sore need of help. I know for a fact Bambi Lovering has entered the pageant. She has a lot of experience. I can teach you how to walk and conduct your interview."

I drained my glass of lemonade, then said, "What's the catch?"

"In exchange for pageant lessons," Miss Odenia said, "I'd like you girls to serve at my card parties on Tuesdays and Fridays. I'm tired of doing all that work myself."

"Serve?" I lifted one eyebrow. I didn't like the sound of this.

"Refreshments," Miss Odenia said.

Handing out cookies at a party didn't sound too bad. "When do we start?"

"Tomorrow at noon. Wear nice clothes. No shorts or T-shirts." She looked pointedly at me. "The lesson will be first. My party is from two to four."

Miss Odenia showed us to the door. Lacey Jane and Rudy burst excitedly outside, but I hung back.

"I'm supposed to babysit Rudy," I said. "What will I do with him tomorrow?"

"Bring him. He can watch TV in my spare room. Or

play in the backyard. You can keep an eye on him." She paused. "What else is troubling you, Rebel?"

I glanced out where Rudy was spinning himself silly. "Why do you *really* want to give us these lessons? Like you said, you don't know me."

She leaned in closer. Her breath smelled like cinnamon. "No, but I do know Lacey Jane. I've watched her grow up. She used to be a happy, sweet child. But after her mama died last winter, that girl's been nothing but a bundle of sorrow."

You could have knocked me over with a wisp of dryer lint. Lacey Jane had never breathed a word about her mother being dead! That explained why she didn't talk about her mother. A pinprick of guilt jabbed my side like a runner's stitch. I felt sorry for her but I didn't want to feel too sorry. It wasn't like we were going to be best friends.

I wondered if I should say anything, and decided right then and there I wouldn't. Lacey Jane would tell me when she was ready. Besides, I felt uncomfortable talking about dead people. Animals dead for thousands of years, no problem. But people—especially somebody's mother— well, that was different.

"Balance on the ball of your foot," Miss Odenia said. "Don't put your heel down first. I know it feels strange, but it's the way pageant girls walk. Try it, Lacey Jane."

Lacey Jane raised up on her toes. "Like this?"

"Not so high."

Lacey Jane took a few wobbly steps. "I keep wanting to put my heel down."

"Practice and you'll get it." Miss Odenia eyeballed me next. "Okay, Rebel. Before you can walk you need to learn correct posture."

Me? Hadn't she seen how Lacey Jane pitched forward like she was dropping off a diving board?

But I sucked my stomach flat to my backbone and stiffened my legs like bed slats. My skirt promptly dropped to the floor in a crumple of denim.

Lacey Jane fell about laughing. "Oh, the judges will *love* that!"

I yanked my skirt back up. "I didn't bring any dresses," I mumbled. "This miniskirt of Lynette's is the only thing that fits. Sort of."

"Is that why you were late?" Lacey Jane asked.

"Mmm-hmm." People didn't need to know *every*thing about me.

"You could've borrowed one of my dresses." Lacey Jane smoothed her bright yellow sundress. Her barrettes and ankle socks matched, natch.

"Mistakes happen even in pageants," Miss Odenia told me. "You picked up your skirt without any fuss, which is good. Now, shoulders back and down. Chin up." She prodded and pulled me into position like a life-size Gumby.

I clutched the counter. "I feel like the Leaning Tower of Pisa!"

"You're not. You're actually standing straight for a change. Okay, girls, one at a time, walk for me. Don't toe out, Rebel. None of that slew-footed business. Make like you're following an invisible line. Long strides. Lift your legs! Point your fingers down—your fingers want to curl naturally, but that doesn't look good."

By the time I pageant-walked from one end of Miss Odenia's living room and back again three times, I had cramps in my calves. Then Lacey Jane took her turn. She turned her toes in so far that her knees locked.

"Again, only this time, smile. Always smile at the judges. You first, Rebel."

I remembered everything she told me—chin up, shoulders down and back, balance on balls of feet, follow invisible line, long strides, fingers pointing down. But I tromped on the back of one of my flip-flops and nearly landed on my face.

"Rebel, you can't wear flip-flops in a pageant." Miss Odenia checked the clock over the stove. "I'll teach you pivot turns tomorrow. Now we need to get ready."

As we fluffed a snowy cloth over the card table and set out hobnail glass luncheon plates, Miss Odenia instructed us to speak politely but only when we're spoken to, serve plates to the left and clear from the right, and serve ice tea to the right. All that nice-manners stuff got on my nerves.

"I wasn't raised in a barn, you know." I glanced out the window to see Rudy, who was supposed to be playing in the backyard, heading for the sewer pipe.

Jerking open the front door, I yelled, "Rudy Parsley, get your scrawny butt *back* in the yard this instant!"

"What on *earth*?" complained a woman teetering at the bottom of the cement steps. "I've never *heard* such screeching!"

It was the lady with the Tastee-Freez hair, three colors swirled on her head like a triple twist cone. Bambi Lovering's mother.

Behind her, two ladies bumped into each other like people in a fire drill. One was decked out in so much costume jewelry, it was a wonder she could stand up. The other had on a flowery pinafore over a white puff-sleeved blouse. Her outfit would have been fine on a nine-year-old, but she had to be pushing fifty.

Miss Odenia hustled me inside. "Go in the kitchen with Lacey Jane and remember what I told you." Then she told her company to come on in.

They clattered into the little hall, jostling pocketbooks and clucking like hens.

"Law," said Jewelry Woman. "I like to melted out there."

"Every bit of the curl fell plumb out of my hair," Pinafore remarked.

"Yes, it's another scorcher. Some ice tea will fix you

right up." Miss Odenia cut her eyes toward me and Lacey Jane.

We poured four glasses and carried them into the living room to the card table. After some backing and filling, Lacey Jane and I figured out how to serve to the right without crashing into each other. Miss Odenia snapped her napkin open in her lap. Our signal to bring in the luncheon plates.

My mouth drooled at the sight of itty-bitty chicken salad and pimento cheese sandwiches in the shape of hearts, spades, diamonds, and clubs, wafer-thin slices of buttered date-nut bread, frosty grapes, and tea cakes dusted with confectioner's sugar.

"Miz Odenia," I whispered as I set her plate down, "can we have the leftovers?" Lynette hadn't gone grocery shopping. For lunch, I'd nibbled a few bites of Rudy's hot dog spaghetti. It was either that or a pine float (glass of water and a toothpick).

"If my guests don't want seconds," she murmured. Fat chance. Those ladies ate like a pack of wolverines. They'd have seconds, all right, and probably lick the dishes sitting in the sink.

Lacey Jane served Bambi's mother with a big smile, but the woman ignored her.

I followed Lacey Jane back into the kitchen and hung over the counter to listen to the ladies gab.

The older woman dressed like a Christmas tree was

86

Viola Sandbanks. She sold Madame Queen costume jewelry. Palmer Sandbanks was her daughter, the famous Palmer who scared the mailman so bad, he stuck the mail in the wrong boxes.

Mimsie Lovering was Bambi's mother, a fact she wouldn't let anyone forget for a second. According to her, Bambi was the prettiest, most talented girl on this planet.

Then I saw a dark brown paw snake out from under the tablecloth. I knew the owner of that foot and prayed it hadn't been splashing in the toilet lately. The paw waved around until its claws snagged the hobnailed edge of Mrs. Lovering's plate and slowly began to pull. I shut my eyes. I couldn't bear to watch.

Mrs. Lovering's scream made my eyes fly open. The plate flipped in her lap, and buttery date-nut bread smeared all over her white dress.

"A rat!" she shrieked, jumping up and scattering the rest of her lunch. Tea cakes, sandwiches, and grapes tumbled on the rug.

The others screamed, too, and hopped up like they were sitting on an anthill.

Doublewide darted out, snatched a club-shaped chicken salad sandwich, and ducked back under the tablecloth. His paw flicked out once more to snick a stray grape.

"What *is* that?" Viola Sandbanks asked, one hand on her chest.

"Lacey Jane, bring me a damp sponge," Miss Odenia

said. "I'm sorry, Mimsie, but I do not have rats." She dabbed at Mrs. Lovering's skirt with the sponge. "There, that's most of it. In this heat, that wet spot will dry in no time." She looked at me. "Who let that lummox of a cat in here?"

"Doublewide must have slipped in when nobody was looking."

"Fetch him and put him outside."

But Doublewide wasn't having any of it. When I raised the tablecloth, he growled and crouched over his sandwich, probably thinking I was going to steal it. Or maybe he was insulted because Bambi's mother had called him a rat.

"He—he's—" I searched for a polite way to say that a stick of dynamite wouldn't budge him. "He's indisposed at the moment."

"Indisposed!" flared Viola Sandbanks. "Well, I never!"

"Let him stay," Palmer said. "Maybe he'll bring me luck."

Miss Odenia said crisply, "Girls, would you clear, please?"

After the last crumb was swept off the tablecloth, Miss Odenia opened a shiny black box and took out a deck of cards.

"Y'all playing poker?" I asked.

"Euchre," said Mimsie Lovering. It sounded like *yuker*.

"Bless you," Lacey Jane said. "Need a Kleenex?"

"That's the name of the *game*."

Miss Odenia expertly dealt the cards, one at a time, around the table, then stacked the leftover cards in the center of the table. "Spades are trump."

"First jack deals," said Palmer, holding up the jack of spades. "Dealers rotate clockwise." She shuffled the leftover deck and began dealing a second round.

Mimsie Lovering talked more than the other three put together. It was Bambi this and Bambi that till I wanted to gag. Or gag *her*. Every time Bambi's name was mentioned, Lacey Jane's lips pursed, and she rattled the dishes.

I didn't know anything about euchre, or whatever it was called, but I noticed that Mimsie Lovering, who sat across from Palmer, gathered the cards after the first game and slung them around. She tossed the last four cards in the center of the table, facedown. They called that pile the kitty.

"Spades trump?" she asked, casually flipping the top card of the kitty. She slid the card into her hand with a satisfied smile.

"Hey," I said. "Isn't it supposed to be Miz Odenia's turn? If you were going clockwise, I mean?"

"Caught stealing the deal, Mimsie Lovering!" Viola Sandbanks exclaimed. "And by somebody who doesn't even know the game!"

"The card's in my hand," Mimsie said tightly. "It's legal."

"*This* time," said Miss Odenia. "Do it again, you'll take a penalty."

Viola waved me over in a jangle of charm bracelets. "Rebel? Would you and Lacey Jane serve at my Madame Queen party tomorrow evening? I'll pay."

Money! I looked at Lacey Jane. She nodded back.

"We'll be there!" I wanted to ask exactly how much she was paying but knew it wasn't polite. Just so long as it was cash on the barrelhead.

I headed back for the kitchen, but Violet Sandbanks grabbed my arm.

"Stay here," she said, "and keep an eye on Mrs. Lovering." She laughed to show she was only joking.

Mimsie Lovering glowered at me. Clearly she was not amused.

The mother of my biggest rival in the beauty pageant was now my enemy.

SEVEN

The Marriage Turtle
of Terrapin Thicket

The card game broke up at exactly four o'clock. Mrs. Lovering opened the door, turning to tell the others good-bye. Rudy, dirty from one end to the other, tried to squeeze inside past her, but stumbled.

"Sorry," he said, slapping grubby handprints on her white dress. "Gotta go to the bathroom."

"Didn't I tell you to stay in the yard?" I said. "You listen real good."

Bambi's mother sniffed. "Were these children raised by cougars?"

At last the company left. Miss Odenia sagged against the wall as Rudy hurled himself into the living room. The hand he'd washed held a tan object.

"Look what I dug out of the ground, Rebel! An old tool from the Cool Age!"

"It's Ice Age, not Cool Age." I examined the pointy object. "Rude, they didn't have plastic knives in the Ice Age with 'Made in China' stamped on them."

"Aw! I thought for sure I found something." He passed it to Lacey Jane. "Want to see?"

She backed away. "Keep your filthy mitts off my brand-clean dress."

"March back into the bathroom," Miss Odenia said to Rudy. "Wash your face and *both* hands. Don't use the little pink towel. That's for good."

Miss Odenia turned on the kitchen faucet, squirted dish soap in the sink, and snapped on a pair of yellow rubber gloves.

"You look like you're in a TV commercial," I told her.

"I *was* in a TV commercial once," she said. "I used to be a hand model."

"Say again?"

"Hand model. That was my job."

"So *that's* why you have all these pictures of hands around," Lacey Jane said.

Miss Odenia dropped silverware into the soapy water. "Those were ads for magazines and newspapers. The statues were cast from my hands. At one time, my hands were kind of famous." She sighed. "But I never got to be an Avon hand model."

Rudy staggered in carrying Doublewide, who was as heavy as a Christmas ham. "Three guesses what I found on the toilet and the first two don't count."

"That cat better not be using my toilet!"

"Be still," I ordered Rudy. "Miz Odenia's about to tell us her life story."

"Y'all don't want to hear about stuff that happened way before you were born."

"Yes, we do!" Lacey Jane and I said at the same time.

Lacey Jane took Miss Odenia's place at the sink. "Rebel and me will clean up."

I didn't sign on to be waitress *and* busboy, but I didn't want to miss this story.

Miss Odenia sank down on the sofa beside Rudy. Doublewide plunked his big self onto her lap, thinking he was forgiven.

"I grew up in Terrapin Thicket. When I was little, I'd sit on the porch with the Sears, Roebuck catalog. I cut out ladies in their evening gowns and day suits and pasted them on corn flakes boxes to make stand-up paper dolls." She rested her head against the back of the sofa and closed her eyes.

"Soon as I could thread a needle, I was sewing my own clothes on Mama's knee-press Singer. I bought material with money I earned working in the garden. No bleached feed sacks for me. Sometimes Ercel Grady—he lived on the next farm—he'd come over and visit. Once he brought me a box turtle he'd found in the garden. I was painting my toenails with Revlon's Cherries in the Snow polish."

I began to wish I hadn't made Miss Odenia tell her life story. Turtles and sewing and paper dolls. Yawn.

"Ercel took the little brush and painted 'EG + OM' on the turtle's back. He liked me and I liked him, but only as a friend. That summer, the Simplicity Pattern Company sent their new spring fashions to our 4-H club. I was one of the girls picked to model the outfits. Oh, how I loved wearing those beautiful dresses. From that second on, I craved to leave Terrapin Thicket and be a fashion model."

"What happened to the turtle?" Rudy asked, bouncing on the cushion.

"Quit interrupting," I said. "And sit still."

"The next summer," Miss Odenia went on, "what should mosey through the garden but that turtle with our initials on its shell? We named him Job because he seemed to be carrying a world of troubles with him. Job came back the next summer too and the summer after that. Ercel said it was a sign that we'd be together forever. I didn't want to get married. I had plans. When I was eighteen, I left home for Washington, D.C. That summer, Job didn't come."

I dried the same lunch plate over and over. Miss Odenia's story wasn't boring anymore. Her low voice almost hypnotized me.

"Modeling agencies didn't want me," she said. "I wasn't tall enough or pretty enough. So I worked as a photographer's secretary. One day he had a job, but the hand model he hired never showed. Then he noticed *my* hands. Next thing I knew, I was holding a Sears iron like I was presenting the crown jewels. Nobody saw my face or my figure. Just my hands."

"This is like a story in a book," Lacey Jane said with a sigh. "Were you rich?"

Miss Odenia smiled. "Hand modeling is hard work. In those days pictures weren't airbrushed. I kept my hands out of the sun so they wouldn't get tan. While I was on the set, I had to hold my arms up in the air to drain the blood. See, blood settles in the hands and makes the blue veins stand out."

All of us except Doublewide checked our hands. My veins were like spiderwebs.

"I took my portfolio of photographs to agencies to get jobs. One day I was at an agency when in comes a woman about my age. The other girls whispered, 'She's the Avon hand model.' Plain as mud with a figure like a scrub board. But her hands were flawless. She never opened doors or windows or cans. She didn't garden or clean. She *always* wore gloves. And she was treated like a queen. I wanted to be a hand model for Avon, like her."

By now I had nearly rubbed a hole in the plate. "Did you get to be one?"

"I moved to New York City. Mama threw her apron over her head. She thought I'd be killed in the big, wicked city. I went on all the casting calls for Avon." Her voice dropped a notch. "But I was never picked. My hands weren't good enough for hand lotion photographs. They were only good enough to push the button on a blender or pour soup in a bowl. Or model gloves. And my hands were cast to use as jewelry store displays."

"But you were famous," I broke in. "How come you're here—" I stopped, realizing that everyone but me lived in Grandview Estates trailer park.

"Living in a mobile home? Never married? No children or grandchildren?" Miss Odenia shook her head. "I lived the life I wanted. I got out of Terrapin Thicket and traveled all over the country. I have no regrets."

Before I could ask what she meant by that, Lacey Jane said, "What happened to Ercel Grady?"

"Mama wrote to me every week faithful," Miss Odenia replied. "She kept me up on the doings back home. Ercel Grady married the Scott girl, Rusleen. They had five children, eleven grandchildren, and six great-grandchildren. Two years ago Ercel sent me a Christmas card. His wife had passed."

"Was it a big funeral?" Rudy butted in. "Open or closed casket? Did a whole bunch of cars drive out to the graveyard? That means the dead person had a lot of friends."

Lacey Jane stared at him. So did I. What was *with* that kid and his obsession with funerals? I dropped my tea towel on the counter and hustled Rudy toward the door. Doublewide jumped off Miss Odenia's lap.

"Time we were getting home," I said, shooing Doublewide ahead of me. "Lynette will worry. Thanks for the lesson, Miz Odenia. See you later, Lacey Jane."

"Thanks for serving," Miss Odenia hollered after me. "Be here tomorrow morning at ten. We'll learn to pivot turn."

The Clunker was parked in the driveway. Its engine cracked and popped in the heat, which meant Lynette had only been home a few minutes. She trudged from the cluster of mailboxes, gripping a fistful of mail.

She fixed me with an angry glare. "I walk in after a long hard day and what do I find? Doublewide's throw-up on the bathroom rug, laundry strung all over the floor, and no supper." Then she noticed Rudy, whose neck, knees, and elbows were caked with dirt. "*Where* have you been?"

"Digging fossils down by the sewer. Rebel and Lacey Jane went to a party," the little snitch replied. I could have throttled him.

"The sewer! You know you're not supposed to go down there! Rebel, why weren't you watching him? What kind of a babysitter are you?"

"The free kind."

Lynette shifted her weight so one hip jutted out. "Well, I'm glad you were having a big time while my son was wallowing in filth."

"I was *not* having a big time, unless you call being a waitress at Miz Odenia's card party a blast," I tossed back.

"I didn't notice Doublewide's accident or I would have cleaned it up. The way that cat eats, no wonder he gets sick. I told Rudy three times to pick up his clothes. And like Old Mother Hubbard said to her dog, the cupboard is bare."

I folded my arms over my chest, daring Lynette to rip into me some more.

But she said, "Shoot. I've been so busy with school I forgot to go grocery shopping. Look, I just got Chuck's check. We'll stop by the bank on the way to Kroger. And I'll fix us a good supper when we get back."

"I want Tater Tots!" Rudy said.

Lynette steered him toward the trailer. "You aren't going anywhere like this."

I hurried in after them, wiping up Doublewide's mess on the rug and collecting Rudy's underwear. Fifteen minutes later, we were tooling down Frog Level Road in The Clunker. Lynette zipped by the drive-up window of the bank, then mashed the gas to Kroger.

"We're all starved cockeyed," she said, swerving into the parking lot. "The absolute worst time to go grocery shopping. Don't buy too much junk."

Even though he was way too old, Rudy hopped into a cart. His knees tucked under his chin, he hung on to the sides as I raced down the aisles. We filled the cart with all sorts of nutritious stuff like Hostess Sno Balls (pink *and* white), Clark bars, Nesquik, and Lucky Charms for Rudy, who finally decided to brave a bowl of cereal for breakfast. I didn't think Lucky Charms was much of an improvement over RC floats, but if he didn't eat it, I would. Gotta love that leprechaun!

We met Lynette at the cookie aisle. Her cart was loaded with soft drinks, grape jelly, peanut butter, saltines, Wonder bread, milk, Velveeta, TV dinners, tuna potpies, and Rudy's Tater Tots.

She eyed the package of pink Sno Balls Rudy was holding. "Rebel, I told you not so much junk."

"Your cart wouldn't win any home ec prizes, either," I said. "We need cookies."

Lynette reached for the two-pound bag of gingersnaps that were on sale.

"Not those," I said hastily. "I don't really like them."

"Then how come you ate a half a bag last night?" Rudy blabbed. "Mama, Rebel stayed in the bathroom a looong time this morning. Doublewide had to go in the yard."

I poked him. "Do we have *any* secrets in this family?"

"And you complain about the way Doublewide eats. I could have told you gingersnaps give you the runs." Lynette set the bag back on the shelf.

I spotted a package of vanilla and chocolate cookies in different shapes. Some were frosted and some were plain. Stella D'Oro Lady Stella assortment. "These look delicioso."

"Four ninety-nine!" Lynette exclaimed when she saw

the price. "Rebel, there are only about twelve cookies in that package."

"With that classy name, they'll be worth it."

While Lynette fixed us a payday supper of tomato soup, grilled cheese sandwiches, and Tater Tots, Rudy and me put the groceries away. I tore the package of Stella D'Oro Lady Stella assortment open.

"Don't spoil your supper," Lynette warned.

"'Life is uncertain. Eat dessert first.' I read that somewhere."

Lynette stirred the soup. "I don't think school will ever get any better. Today Marcie—her station is next to mine—she begged me to cut her hair. She knows we're only allowed to work on our mannequin heads. But she went on so, I took her in the break room and gave her a haircut."

"Did she like it?" I bit into a white-iced chocolate cookie.

"Are you kidding? She said it looked like I used a chain saw. I told her she didn't have the kind of hair for a choppy bob, but did she listen? So now Marcie's telling the other girls I ruined her hair on purpose."

"Sic Lacey Jane on her. She'll straighten her out," I said.

"Speaking of Lacey Jane," Lynette said to me, "what were you and her up to today?"

"We served the food and washed the dishes at Miz

Odenia's card party." The chocolate cookie didn't have much taste. I nibbled on a square pink-frosted vanilla.

Lynette pretended to reel backward. "If I ask you to pick a poppy seed off the floor, you whine and carry on something awful. And you're serving and washing dishes for Miz Matthews?"

The pink-frosted cookie wasn't any better. I tried a plain round vanilla. "Every day you tell me stuff to do and I do it, plus watch Rudy, which isn't the easiest job in the world."

"Hey!" he protested.

Lynette took the pan off the burner and poured the soup into two bowls, flipped our sandwiches over, and checked the Tater Tots in the oven. I marveled that she could do all of those things at once. I could pour the soup or flip the sandwiches or open the oven door, but only one thing at a time. Even then I'd probably mess up.

"You know why I was working at Miz Odenia's today?" I asked her.

"I've been waiting."

"She's teaching us how to be beauty pageant contestants."

"Say what?" A grilled cheese sandwich leaped out of the skillet. Lynette didn't even bother to scrape it off the floor.

"You heard right. Lacey Jane and me entered the Frog Level firemen's carnival beauty pageant." I didn't tell her

I borrowed the entry fee. Or that I forged her signature on the form. "Miz Odenia is showing us how to walk right. She was once—well, she knows about that stuff. In exchange, me and Lacey Jane serve at her parties."

Rudy piped up. "Miz Odenia told us a story about a turtle she was gonna marry."

Lynette didn't even hear that ridiculous remark. "I can't believe you *of all people* entered a *beauty pageant*!"

I shrugged. "It's something to do." Like heck it was. I'd commit capital murder to get to that paleontology dig.

Lynette came over and lifted my hair off my neck. "We should definitely put your hair up. With a few curls off to one side. And of course I'll do your makeup."

I pushed her hand away. "No makeup. And no weird hairdos, Miss Chain Saw Stylist. I want to look like myself."

She gave my shoulder a little slap. "I ought to snatch you bald-headed for that remark. And if you look like yourself, you can forget about winning."

"The Stella D'Oro cookie people lied," I said, shoving the bag across the table. "This isn't an assortment. The cookies *look* different but they all taste the same."

Lynette brought over our plates. "Cookies are a lot like life, Rebel. A lot of it tastes the same."

I had no idea what she was talking about. But then, my sister and me didn't seem like we came from the same family, most of the time.

Bambi Lovering's
EXPERT BEAUTY TIPS

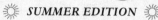

☀ *SUMMER EDITION* ☀

---

*Y*ou don't have to go through life with "rabbit lashes." Yes, Rebel McKenzie, this means you! Don't walk around another second with eyeballs like olives in a jar. Take action now!

Beef up puny eyelashes in five easy steps:

1. Sleep on your back, not your stomach! Your eyes get all mashed in the mattress. See those little tiny hairs on the pillowcase? Bye-bye eyelashes.

2. Grease your eyelashes with Vaseline right before bedtime. It makes them grow longer and thicker.

3. Don't rub your eyes! You pull out precious lashes.

4. Use an eyelash curler. Place the curler part where your eyelashes grow out of your eyelids. Close the handle. Don't squeeze too hard!

5. Get out your trusty Vaseline. Sprinkle a little baby powder on your eyelashes. Add a teeny dab of Vaseline. Your eyelashes will look thicker and shinier instantly. And you have *me* to thank for it!

Until next time . . . smile pretty!

*B*ambi Lovering,
Your Expert Beauty Consultant

Rudy and the Hand Monstur

EIGHT

Kissy

Before my eyelids cracked open, I heard somebody banging on the front door. I waited to see if Lynette would get it, but after the fourth set of bangs, I stumbled out of bed and into the hall. Since I was still wearing my daddy's T-shirt that I sleep in, I unlocked the door and opened it just a sliver.

"It's me," Lacey Jane said, bright as a new dime in a red-and-white shorts set even though the sun had barely peeped over the 7-Eleven. "Take this. And this." She handed me a large brown cat and a folded piece of pink paper.

Doublewide lay heavily across my outstretched arms like a two-ton rag doll. The paper was bunched up in one hand, so I couldn't read it.

"Why are you bringing us our cat?" I asked. "We already know he lives here, unfortunately."

"Tell *him* that," Lacey Jane said. "Daddy just came home, mad enough to bust. He was almost to work when this big ol' thing jumped in the front seat."

"The cat rides in cars?"

She nodded. "It's not the first time Doublewide went to sleep in the back of Daddy's van. Daddy said it better be the last. Did you know he used to pretend he was homeless and begged for table scraps? Doublewide, I mean. Not my daddy."

I dropped Doublewide—*ker-plunk*—on the floor. He ran off to investigate his food dish. "What's the paper?"

"I found it stuck in your door. I didn't read it, but I bet I know what it is."

It took me four seconds to scan the latest edition of *Bambi Lovering's Expert Beauty Tips*. Then I crumpled the paper in a tight ball, wishing it was Bambi's head.

"Don't tell me you're cursed with a beauty defect too," Lacey Jane guessed.

"Rabbit lashes." I blinked several times to make my eyelashes flutter. They were *not* puny.

Lacey Jane laughed. "*Rabbit lashes!* Next you'll have guinea pig lips!"

"You didn't think it was so funny when she said you had piano legs." The more I thought about Bambi's nerve, the hotter I got.

"Oh, good, you're up." Lynette rushed into the hall. She saw Lacey Jane and said, "Hey there, Lacey Jane."

Today Lynette wore her hair in a towering heap that defied gravity. A smooth layer covered the snarled teased part, like a sheet thrown over a brush pile.

"Rebel," she said, grabbing a banana from the wooden bowl on the counter, "I'm late. Will you make my bed? Ta-ta!" With a waggle of her fingers, she was out the door. No wonder she was late. It must have taken hours to back-comb her hair into a skyscraper.

"'Will you make my bed?'" I mocked Lynette's new, mincing beauty-school voice. "'And cook ten-course meals and rearrange the gravel in the driveway with twee-zers?' What I really want to do is give Bambi a gigantic Dutch rub."

"Get your chores over with first," Lacey Jane said. "That's what I do."

I looked at her. This was the first time she'd admitted that she did the housework now. It was a good moment to tell her I knew about her mother. Then Rudy came in.

"Hey, Lacey Jane," he said. "Hey, Rebel. Where's Mama?"

"She left already." My mad was not going away. I had to do something before I exploded. "Rudy, go watch car-toons. I'll be back in a few minutes."

"Where're you going?"

"Just across the street. I'll be right back. Don't get into anything. Okay?"

"'kay."

Lacey Jane tried to stop me. "Rebel, you're still in your nightclothes!"

"So what? Bambi Lovering has messed with the wrong person." I pushed her aside and marched across the street.

Lacey Jane's sandals clip-clipped behind me. Rudy straggled behind her, and Doublewide brought up the rear. Nothing like leading a parade.

Hopping up the cement steps, I leaned on the Loverings' doorbell. The door jerked open so fast, I nearly fell inside.

Bambi stood there in a purple bathrobe with glittery stars. A pink satin mask was pushed up on her forehead.

"Kind of early for Halloween, isn't it?" I said. "Or are you on your way to rob a bank?"

"This is an *eye* mask, I'll have you know. What are y'all doing here at this unearthly hour?"

"I got your beauty tip," I began. "Here's what I think of—"

Yarkyarkyarkyarkyark!

Something very small, very furry, and very fast launched itself at me. Pin-sharp teeth locked on my ankle. I lifted my foot, but the critter hung on, growling.

"Kissy!" Bambi picked up a wriggling tan-and-silver fur ball and tucked it under her chin. "Is that any way to behave? No attacking, not even if Rebel deserves it."

"It's a *dog*," Rudy cried. "Aw, isn't it cute! When'd you get it?"

"Yesterday," Bambi said, stroking Kissy's licorice-drop nose. "I bought her with my Miss John Deere prize money. She's a Yorkie—Yorkshire terrier. She'll only weigh about five pounds when she's full-growed."

"You named her Kissy?" Lacey Jane asked.

"Yeah, 'cause all I want to do is kiss this sweet li'l thing. *Mwa, mwa, mwa, mmm-wa!*" Bambi plastered lip-smackers all over the poor dog's fuzzy little head.

Rudy held out his arms. "Can I hold her?" he asked, lovesick over both Bambi and her scrap of a dog.

She looked at him. "You have a giant booger in your nose."

"And you've got a big stick up your butt," I said, as Rudy turned away, his shoulders slumping. "Where do you get off telling people about their rabbit lashes and boogers?"

"'Good grooming habits are the way to start your day,'" she returned. "That's from chapter two of the beauty advice book I'm writing."

"Are you for real? I bet your mama ordered you from the Sears catalog."

Doublewide sidled by my leg, staring up at Kissy, probably thinking it was a long-haired rat. Doublewide easily made three of that dog.

Kissy wiggled out of Bambi's grip and skittered over to the cat. *Yarkyarkyarkyarkyarkyarkyark!*

"Shoo!" I said to the dog. "Go on!" The last thing

I needed was a fight around my sore heels. "Grab your stupid dog before she gets hurt!"

"You better be worrying about the cat," Bambi yelled over Kissy's barking. "Kissy is a terrier. She's not afraid of anything."

Doublewide watched nonchalantly as Kissy raced around in tight circles. Then he drew himself up, waited until the dog was within swatting range, and—*thwack!*—boxed Kissy with his Brontotherium-sized paw. Squealing, the dog rolled over like a sow bug.

Bambi snatched Kissy up. "Get that big bully out of here!"

I stuck my face close to Bambi's. "I know you think you're greatest thing since sliced bread, but get ready. Me and Lacey Jane entered the firemen's carnival pageant. In the same category as you."

"Oh, please," she said with a harsh laugh. "You two will *never* be in the same category as me."

"Better take your own beauty advice," Lacey Jane said. "You finally have serious competition."

We walked back across the street, satisfied. Me in my sleep-shirt, Lacey Jane in her red shorts and matching ankle socks and barrettes, Rudy in his NASCAR pajamas, Doublewide padding along, his round stomach swaying.

Rudy thoughtfully worked his finger up his nose to the second joint.

"Rude," I said, "wait till we're home before you clean the bat out of the cave."

"My knees hurt," I complained to Lacey Jane as I scattered Ritz crackers on a silver tray. "This gig better pay good."

"Because you did the pivot turns wrong. Rebel, don't dump stuff on the tray. Fix it nice."

"Why? They'll just mess it up. Remember how these ladies eat?"

For the second time in two days, me and Lacey Jane were serving food. This time at Viola Sandbanks's Madame Queen jewelry party. And for the second time in two days, me and Lacey Jane had had a pageant lesson from Miss Odenia.

This morning, Miss Odenia showed us how to do this neat turn at the end of our pageant walk. You place one foot in front of the other, raise your heels, and spin so you're facing the other way. The foot that was behind is now in front, and you walk back in the direction you came.

Unless you're me and you turn the wrong way so your knees crash into each other.

"Right foot first," Miss Odenia kept telling me. "Pivot to the left. Your *other* left."

Lacey Jane pivoted like she was on roller skates at the end of her walk, and even in the middle of her walk, while I had to have Miss Odenia pry my legs apart with a soup ladle. At the end of our lesson, I could barely crawl home.

Viola Sandbanks sailed into the kitchen, no small feat since she wore at least sixty-five pins on the front of her dress. Swags of pearls and beads swung out from her bosom, and bracelets were stacked clear up to her elbow.

When she moved, she clacked and clanked like the Tin Man. Now I know why she asked us to serve. Weighed down with all that jewelry, she couldn't pick up a marshmallow.

"How we doing, girls? Lacey Jane, that cookie platter is simply lovely." She frowned at my cracker tray.

"I saw this in the latest *Good Housekeeping*," I fibbed. You dump out a whole box of crackers. It's called The Volcano."

"Really? Well, if it's the latest—"

Palmer Sandbanks fluttered in. She had rings on every finger, even her thumbs. "Mama, everybody's coming up the walk."

"Let them in, dear." To us, Viola said, "Make the punch, girls. The recipe is on the counter." She clanked into the living room.

"Volcano. What a crock," Lacey Jane said, pouring ginger ale into the huge glass bowl. "How much cranberry juice do I add?"

I glanced at the stained index card. "Six quarts."

Craning my neck, I saw Miss Odenia with Mrs. Randolph, the old lady from Better-Off-Dead Pest Control and Bridal Consignment. Right behind them strutted Bambi's mother . . . and Bambi herself, decked out in a pink polka-dot sundress. She carried Kissy in a wicker basket. The dog sported a pink rhinestone collar.

"Six? That sounds like a lot." Lacey Jane began taking bottles from the fridge.

"Guess who's here?"

"Not the Scourge of Grandview Estates?"

"In the pink," I said. "Complete with dog."

Bambi heard our voices. She whispered something to her mother, then hiked her nose in the air.

Viola clapped loudly. "Ladies, I want to call your attention to the new arrivals in the Madame Queen collection on the coffee table. Black-and-white enamel is all the go this summer."

"Oooh, I'm gonna get me that black-and-white daisy brooch," Palmer gushed. "Mr. Beechley won't be able to take his eyes off me."

"Palmer, I've told you a thousand times to stop chasing after the mailman," her mother said. "If he was interested in you, he'd have asked you out by now."

"He's just a slow mover. He'll come around," Palmer said, unfazed.

I rolled my eyes at Lacey Jane. Poor Mr. Beechley. I wondered why he didn't quit being a mailman and take up a safer job, like Hollywood stuntman.

"You'll have time to look at the samples during refreshments," Viola said. "Let's play a game to break the ice."

What ice? It was five hundred degrees outside. Plus, everybody knew each other.

"Palmer, pass out the tablets and pencils. Ladies, see how many words you can make from 'Madame Queen.' The winner gets the door prize," Viola said grandly.

"How many words are there?" Miss Odenia asked.

"I found twenty," Palmer replied.

I flipped the recipe card over and grabbed a pen. "Does 'Madame' have an 'e'?"

"Yes," Lacey Jane said. "Put down 'queen.' And 'madam.'"

"Duh." I scribbled furiously. This was one game I was good at. *Mad. Dam. Dean. Meat. An. Ad. Ma. Am. Need.*

"'Deem'?" Lacey Jane suggested. "Is that a word?"

"Yes indeedy!" My pen flew. *Name. Made. Man. Men. Den. Due.*

"Time's up!" Viola chirped. "Who got ten words?" Everyone raised their hands. "Twelve?" Miss Odenia's hand went down. "Thirteen?" Mrs. Randolph dropped out.

"I have fourteen," said Mimsie Lovering. "But my princess has a big long list."

"Did you get all twenty, Bambi?" Viola asked.

Bambi flashed her tablet. "Yes! I won!"

"No, you didn't!" I stormed into the living room waving the index card. "*I* got twenty-*two*."

"The help isn't allowed to play!" Bambi protested.

"Girls, let's be nice." Viola read Palmer's list, then mine, then Bambi's.

"'Que' is not a word!" I said, pointing at Bambi's babyish printing.

"Is too," Bambi tossed back.

"Is not."

Palmer checked the dictionary. "Rebel's right. There's no such word as 'que.' At least not spelled that way."

"Rebel is not in the game," said Bambi's mother. "Bambi still has nineteen words. She wins."

I guess Palmer and Viola figured Mimsie Lovering was good for a big sale and I wasn't. Palmer handed Bambi a silver charm in the shape of a dog.

"Oooh! It's perfect!" Bambi squealed.

"I wonder what a *liar* charm would look like?" I whispered loudly to Lacey Jane.

Viola snapped her fingers. "Bring the refreshments now."

We took in the snack plates first. Then we hauled in the sloshing punch bowl.

"Ewww," Bambi remarked. "That looks like blood!"

Viola took us aside. "How much cranberry juice did you put in?"

"Six quarts. Like the recipe said," I replied.

"It's supposed to be three!" Veins pulsed in her temples.

I shrugged. "Can I help it the card was smudgy? Say

it's lava punch to go with the cracker volcano."

Lacey Jane passed the chips and dip to Bambi's mother. "Your hair looks pretty tonight," she said shyly.

Mrs. Lovering fluffed the ruffle on Bambi's dress and didn't answer. The corners of Lacey Jane's mouth turned down. Suddenly I realized why Lacey Jane hated Bambi so much, aside from the obvious fact that Bambi was a horrible human being. Bambi's mother fussed over her constantly. Lacey Jane's father worked all the time. Nobody made over Lacey Jane anymore.

"Punch?" I offered a brimming cup to Bambi.

As she reached for it, I put my right foot in front of my left, lifted my heels, and twirled in a perfect pivot turn. Then I pivoted again so I was facing her, accidentally-on-purpose tipping the punch down the neck of her sundress.

"Oh my! How *clumsy* of me."

Miss Odenia, who had seen the whole thing, gasped. "Rebel!"

Bambi sprang up. "Mama! Look what she did! I'm soaking wet!" She began to cry huge crocodile tears.

Mrs. Lovering glowered at me. "I don't want to see you at another party!" She swept Bambi into the bathroom. When they came out ten minutes later, Bambi's dress was still stained. "I'll send you my dry-cleaning bill," she told Viola Sandbanks.

"Wait, Mama," Bambi said, still sniveling. "Can I have that blue stone bracelet?"

"Of course, baby. How about one for Kissy so you'll be twins?"

Bambi smiled, showing all of her teeth and forty-eleven dimples.

After the party, Lacey Jane and me poured about hundred gallons of punch down the sink. Nobody drank it, for some reason. When we were ready to go, I asked Viola about our payment.

"Here," she said. Two plain fake-gold pins clattered on the counter, the cheapest of all the Madame Queen jewelry.

"Um," I said. "I was hoping for cash." Like, at least five dollars.

"After the shenanigans you pulled? Take the pins or nothing."

We took and left. Our paid serving career was over.

When we reached our street, I walked over to the Loverings' house.

"What are you doing?" Lacey Jane asked.

"Something." I dug in my pocket for my Madame Queen list and the pencil I'd swiped. One word on my list hadn't been on Palmer's or Bambi's.

I circled the word *mean* and slipped the paper under the door.

From the Field Notebook
of Rebel McKenzie

The Gobi Desert is brutal in July. All you see is sand, sand, and more sand. The sky is white, the sand is white, and the sun is round and red like a jawbreaker.

I am working on a grinding tooth of a woolly mammoth. Mammoths were—well, mammoth—big, and needed to eat a lot of grass and leaves and stuff. Their teeth had ridges that helped them chew plants.

This tooth was attached to a boulder way down deep. I chipped at the rock with my hammer and chisel. My kneepads were scorching.

My chisel hit something. I stopped to look at it through my magnifying glass. Smoke poured between my fingers. It was so hot, my magnifying glass had set the rock on fire!

A shadow fell over my dig site. A vulture, waiting until I keeled over. It wouldn't be long now. . . .

NINE

Christmas Lights in July

*"**F**olks, it's gonna be hotter'n a two-dollar pistol today. All you sugar
boogers out there, stay cool. Put a tub of ice in front of your fan
and lap up the breeze, but don't twitch your dial from WKCW—"*

"Lynette, cut that stupid radio off. The guy's making
me sweat just listening to him." My voice echoed off the
bathroom tile.

I lolled on the bathroom floor, the coolest place in the
trailer, my head propped on *The How and Why Wonder Book
of Prehistoric Mammals.* I had on a halter top and short-shorts.
Baby powder coated me from my forehead to my toenails.
I lay motionless as an amoeba in a coma, but heat still radi-
ated from me. You could deep-fry okra on my stomach.

Lynette's bare feet slapped into the bathroom. "You
look like you've been dipped in Shake 'N Bake." She sat
down on the closed toilet seat and opened her cosmetology

book. Then she slammed it shut. "I don't want to study scabies and impetigo today."

"Who would? Why do you need to learn that gross stuff for anyway?"

"Some skin diseases are contagious. If somebody wants their hair done and they have scabies, I tell them they should go to a doctor. And that I'm not allowed to work on them. I might catch it."

"See, this is why I like paleontology. The animals are already dead and I can't catch anything."

Rudy scooted into the bathroom, shirtless and barefoot. A wicked heat rash blotched his chest.

"Look," he said, holding up an outdoor thermometer. "The red thing is all the way at the top!"

I sat up. Baby powder sifted from my arms. "Where did you have that thing?"

"On the front steps. What's it say, Rebel?"

"A hundred and forty degrees." My eyes popped out. "Lynette, it's a *hundred* and forty *degrees* and we don't have a *speck* of air-conditioning."

"Rebel, he set the thermometer in the sun." She tugged the rubber band from her ponytail, gathered up her hair, and pulled it into a higher ponytail. "I don't have the money to get the A/C fixed, you know that. The man said I need a whole new compressor or whatever, and I can't afford it."

"Can you afford a paper fan?" I knew money was

tight, but it was just too hot to live.

"Quit it, Rebel. Just quit it." Then she said to Rudy, "Snooty-kins, you aren't supposed to be out in the sun. It'll make your rash worse. Let me put some more powder on you." She frowned at my flour-white legs. "If Rebel hasn't used it all."

"Here." I tossed the mostly-empty can of baby powder to her. Rudy stood still while she sprinkled his chest. I opened my book and tried to read, but the words squiggled in front of my eyes like tadpoles.

"You're always dragging that book around," Lynette said. "It looks boring."

"Not as boring as your ol' cosmetology book. I help you study all those yucky diseases and body parts, but you don't know a thing about the Ice Age."

"I wished I lived in it," she said. "The Ice Age would feel good right about now. Rebel, is that my halter top?"

"I don't know. Is it?"

"You know it is. No wonder I couldn't find it." She fanned herself with her cosmetology book, scattering baby powder. Rudy sneezed.

"Are we going to spend all day in this teeny little bathroom?" I asked in disgust. "I can't wait for the first day of school. My essay will be called 'How I Spent My Summer Vacation Holed Up in a Bathroom of a Trailer.'"

"Don't call my house a trailer," Lynette said.

"Excuuuse me! The *mobile home* you rent."

"Don't fight," Rudy said. "It makes my liver hurt." Whenever I helped Lynette study anatomy, he hung on every organ. He pointed at the cover of my book. "What's that animal?"

"Baluchitherium." I sounded out the word slowly. "*Ba-luck-uh-THEE-re-um*. It was twenty-three feet tall! A Baluchitherium could eat the tops of trees."

"Bad-luck-a-theem," Rudy repeated softly, slaughtering the pronunciation.

Lynette twisted her mouth. "Ba-luck-a-duck, my foot. You're making that up."

"I am not, you Neanderthal," I said under my breath.

"I heard that. You think you're so smart. I'll find you in *my* book." Furiously, she flipped the pages of her cosmetology book.

"Go ahead. Whatever you find, I'll pick out a better one that's you."

"Acne pustulosa." She held up the book so I could see the picture of an oozing sore. "'The variety of acne in which pustular lesions are present.' That's you."

"Ewww! Gross!" Rudy sounded delighted.

"Is that so?" I didn't even need to look through my book. "Page thirty-one."

Lynette found the page. "A—barylamda." She glared at me. "I do *not* have a thick, heavy reptilian tail!"

"Yes, you do. Plus a short, blunt face so you can grub for roots," I said, cackling.

"It's a long walk back home to Mama's—"

"You called me pus head!"

Lynette set our books on the edge of the sink. "You know what? I got seventeen dollars in tips last week. I was gonna put it on the light bill, but I think we need to buy a couple of fans."

"Yay!" I jumped up in a shower of powder.

I thought we'd head to Sears or True Value Hardware, but Lynette drove The Clunker in the opposite direction. We pulled into the parking lot of Bargain Bin, part flea market, part "junktiques."

"You can't get fans here. You have to go to a hardware store," I said, ungluing myself from the hot duct-taped seat and leaving behind most of my skin.

"You can get anything here."

"Look, Mama!" Rudy exclaimed. "There's a little girl for sale! She's only four dollars. Let's buy her!"

"Rude, that kid is not for sale," I told him. "She's holding a sign for that extremely ugly lamp."

Lynette was right. You *could* get anything at Bargain Bin, including a lamp made out of a globe sawed in half, fringed with glass beads, and stuck on a large brass dolphin.

The inside of Bargain Bin was dim and smelled like potatoes stored too long. The place was jammed floor to ceiling with boxes and cartons and bags of stuff. Musty paperbacks spilled from milk crate bookcases. Kitchen utensils were tangled in mildewed doilies. Now I knew where the Hula-Hoop went to die.

"How can we find anything in this mess?" I said to Lynette.

"Split up. We'll cover more ground that way. Rudy, you want to come with me or Rebel?"

He thought a few seconds, as if choosing between a solid-gold wristwatch and a Shetland pony. "Rebel," he said at last.

"Rebel, look for box fans—they sit on the floor. Seven dollars, tops." She disappeared down a junk-filled aisle.

"Okay, Rudy. Let's go this way." As we stepped carefully around rusted old tools, I couldn't decide which we needed more, tetanus shots or a compass.

But at the end of the aisle sat a twenty-six-inch box fan, still in its original carton. The price on the neon sticker—six-fifty. Score!

The fan wasn't heavy, but the box was bulky. Me and Rudy carried it to the front, where a man in a greasy pony-tail munched Doritos and squinted at a gecko race on one of those teeny little TV sets. No, those were horses, not geckos.

"Can we leave this here?" I asked him. "We're still shopping."

"Yeah, sure." He didn't pull his eyes from the TV screen.

We met Lynette in a section of mismatched dishes. She had a floor fan tucked under one arm.

"Five bucks," she said. I told her about my bargain.

"Good deal, Reb! We have a little money left over. What do you think of this?" She tugged a child's plastic wading pool from under a shelf. It was filled with spiders, some dead, others crawling up the sloping sides.

"Starting a spider farm?" I asked.

"Very funny. We'll put it in the yard and take turns sitting in it. It even comes with an inner tube."

"Lynette, even Rudy doesn't fit in that pool. We'll look like idiots."

"Who cares? At least we'll be cool."

Was this my sister? The one who wouldn't fetch the mail unless she had on mascara and an ankle bracelet?

"Oh, boy!" Rudy cried. "We can go swimming!"

If you call sitting in a teacup of water *swimming*.

"The pool is only two dollars," Lynette said. "That's—um—thirteen-fifty. We still have a few bucks left. Why don't y'all pick something out for yourself?"

"There really isn't anything I want in this place." *But you can give me the cash for my Kids' Dig trip*, I nearly added.

"Go with Rudy, then. I'll meet you at the checkout."

"Yay! I know just what I want!" Rudy dashed off. I found him on his knees rummaging through an old suitcase overflowing with worn leashes and dog collars.

"Rude, we don't have a dog."

"Ta-da!" He pulled out a red rhinestone-studded collar that looked brand new. "Bambi's dog has a fancy collar, and Doublewide should too."

I examined the collar. "It's for a medium-sized dog, so it should go around that cat's lardy neck. And it's only fifty cents."

"Okay, I got my thing. What're you gonna get, Rebel?"

"They don't have a meat freezer with a built-in bed. That's all I want—" Then my gaze lit on a brown furry ball. "Look, Rudy, a head made out of a coconut! It even has real teeth! Shoot, it costs eight bucks."

But under the coconut head was something I liked even better. And it only cost seventy-five cents. We took our prizes to the front, where Lynette paid for everything.

At home, Lynette set both fans in the living room and switched them on "high." "At night we'll each have a fan in our bedroom."

Rudy jerked Doublewide from a sound sleep on the back of the sofa and clasped the fake ruby collar around his neck.

Doublewide blinked twice. Then he arched his back and bucked like a steer. He rolled and romped and stood on his head. He shook his head until his eyes were a blue blur and scratched behind his ears so hard he fell over.

"Rudy, for heaven's sake, the cat hates that collar," Lynette said. "Take it off."

"He'll get used to it."

Doublewide pushed himself along the carpet with his hind feet, trying to get rid of the collar. He was *not* getting used to it. Finally he sat on the floor, flicking the end of his tail, his ears flat like airplane wings.

"Put your bathing suits on, everybody!" Lynette said. "The pool is about to open!"

While she and Rudy were out back, I took my package from the wrinkled grocery bag Ponytail Man had put it in.

When I went outside, Lynette oozed half in and half out of the wading pool like a fish too big for the skillet, her head resting on the inner tube. She dribbled water over her shoulders.

"Ahhh. This is the life." She lifted an invisible glass. "Waiter, I'll have another mint julep."

Rudy danced in the puddle left by the dripping hose. "Rebel, are you gonna show Mama what you bought?"

"I'm putting them up now." I opened the package and took out a long string of tiny white Christmas tree lights.

Standing on an upturned bucket, I draped the string of lights around the window. The cord just reached the outlet. I plugged the lights in, and the window glowed firefly-shiny.

"Oooh," Rudy said. "It looks just like Christmas."

I put my hands on my hips and smiled at the twinkling lights. "That's the idea. Christmas is the coolest thing I can think of."

"Good gravy," Lynette said. "Christmas lights! Could we be any tackier?"

"It makes our house pretty," Rudy declared.

"Mobile home," I corrected.

Doublewide came out to see what the fuss was about. He walked a little sideways, still not used to the dog collar. He glanced up at the lights, yawned, then sniffed the box, hoping it contained a few grains of cat chow.

"Do you know an old-timey animal name for Doublewide?" Rudy asked. "Like you and Mama called each other."

"You mean prehistoric?" I thought a minute. "How about *Megalonyx doublewidus*? It weighed thirty-five hundred pounds."

"That's our cat!" Rudy said proudly.

Lynette splashed her feet. "I guess we have arrived. A kid's wading pool to cool off in and Christmas lights in July. We are truly members of the trailer-park set."

"You said it, Barylambda. Feels good to get your reptile tail wet, doesn't it?"

I didn't duck quick enough.

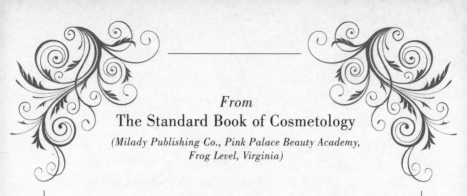

From
The Standard Book of Cosmetology
*(Milady Publishing Co., Pink Palace Beauty Academy,
Frog Level, Virginia)*

The Successful Cosmetologist

Good habits and practices will lay the foundation for a successful career in cosmetology. A successful cosmetologist should:

1. *M*ake good impressions on others and cultivate the qualities of charm, confidence, and personality.

2. *P*ractice wholesome, healthy thoughts.

3. *B*e neat, clean, and attractive.

4. *H*ave a sunny disposition.

5. *P*ractice good ethics: honesty, fairness, courtesy, and respect for the rights and feelings of others.

TEN

Friday Night's Dream

"Personally, I think Miz Odenia's standards are slipping," I said to Lacey Jane as we headed down the street, clinging to patchy shade.

It was Saturday, hot as blue blazes. Lynette was off from school and work, so Rudy had stayed with her.

I went on with my complaint. "The food we served at her card party yesterday was terrible. Canned soft drinks. Peanuts. Vanilla *wafers*. At her other party, she fixed fancy sandwiches and tea cakes."

"You didn't notice it was stuff we couldn't spill?" Lacey Jane said. "Miz Odenia probably doesn't trust us. And after the way you spied on Bambi's mother, I'm surprised she still wants to give us pageant lessons."

"Bambi's mother cheats," I said. "She acts like butter won't melt in her mouth, but she's a card cheat."

Miss Odenia was pulling weeds in her zinnia border. When she saw us, she stood and waved. "'Morning, girls."

"'Morning. Are we gonna practice walking and turning today?" I asked, following Miss Odenia into her trailer.

"I think you have pivot turns down," Miss Odenia replied wryly. Obviously she hadn't forgotten the neat pivot I had done at Viola Sandbanks's party. "Today we're going to work on the talent part of the pageant."

An old-fashioned record player was set up on her coffee table. I flipped through her collection of record albums.

"I never heard of any of these people," I said.

"That's good, isn't it?" Lacey Jane asked Miss Odenia. "Bambi sings an old-timey song and the judges like it."

Miss Odenia nodded. "Bambi also plays an unusual instrument. Harpists and violinists are often in the top ten. Pageant judges like to see a show. You need to stand out. Be unique."

"Unique like play the ukulele behind your head?" I said. No way was I going to do anything that stupid.

"Make fun of Bambi all you want, but she has a nice voice. Her mother was in the Sweet Adelines. Singers connect better with audiences." Miss Odenia put a record on the turntable. Judy Garland's "Over the Rainbow" flowed out of the speaker. "Lacey Jane, sing along, please."

"What? Really? Okay." Lacey Jane clasped her hands together and belted out, *"Some-WHERE O-ver the rain-BOOOWW, Way UP hiiiigh—"*

Miss Odenia made chopping motions with her hand. "Lacey Jane, you aren't even on key. Rebel, you try."

I tried to figure out where Lacey Jane went wrong. Maybe she was loud in the wrong places. *"SOME-wherrrre o-VERRR the rain-BOOOOOWW, WAAAY up—"*

Miss Odenia lifted the needle so fast, she scratched her record. "Maybe I'm going at this backward. Tell me what talents you have. Rebel?"

"I have *lots* of talents," I said, as if I had to wade through drifts of blue ribbons just to go brush my teeth. "I can hear like a dog and read things upside down and I'm a very good observer. Plus, I'm a paleontologist."

And an expert belch-talker, but Mama always said it didn't pay to brag too much.

"Hmmm. Those are all interesting abilities, Rebel, but kind of hard to perform onstage. Do you play a musical instrument?"

"No."

Lacey Jane raised her eyebrows. "What about that you-phone thing?"

I had to think what she meant. "Oh! The eu*phonium.* I'm really not that good."

Miss Odenia turned to Lacey Jane. "What about you?"

Lacey Jane dug the toe of her sandal into the rug. "I don't have a lick of talent. When we put on plays in school, I always paint the sets."

Miss Odenia put her arm around Lacey Jane's shoulders.

"Everyone has a natural gift in something. It just needs to be brought out. Sit down and think about what you'd like to do. I'll work with Rebel first."

"I can do anything," I said, practically quivering with talent. "Except play the ukulele behind my head. I mean, I can. I just won't."

"Because you like to *talk* a lot," Miss Odenia broke in, "I think you should do a recitation of a poem."

"You want me to tell a *poem* for my talent?"

"Not tell, recite. Act it out dramatically. Watch me do 'The Raven' by Edgar Allan Poe. 'Once upon a midnight dreary—'" She hunched over like a witch. "'While I pondered weak and weary, over many a quaint and curious volume of forgotten lore.'" She nodded over an invisible book. "'While I nodded, nearly napping, suddenly there came a tapping.'" She looked up sharply, as if she heard someone knocking.

"Where's the poem at?" asked Lacey Jane. "I don't see you reading it."

"You memorize it. I still remember the poetry I recited when I was a girl. 'The Raven.' 'The Village Blacksmith.' 'Hiawatha.'"

Miss Odenia doubled over suddenly. I thought she might be having a spasm, but she was laughing.

"In fourth grade, I got up to recite 'The Village Blacksmith,' and my mind went blank as a slate! I could only remember the first line. 'Under a spreading chestnut tree, the village smithy stands.' And stands and stands and stands and stands, and stands and stands and *stands*."

"So what poem do you want me to recite?" I asked, not much liking this talent.

She handed me a book called *Complete American Poems*. "Pick out something by Longfellow. Not 'Hiawatha.' Everybody knows that one." Everybody but me. "Try 'Evangeline' or 'Paul Revere's Ride.'"

"I figured out what I want to do," Lacey Jane announced, sliding off the sofa. "I want to dance."

"An interpretive dance!" Miss Odenia exclaimed. "Good choice! Put a song on the record player and start moving the way the music makes you feel."

Lacey Jane pulled out a record with a brown-haired woman on the cover. "This one," she said, pointing to the list on the back.

"'Sweet Dreams' by Patsy Cline? Do you know this song?" Miss Odenia asked.

"No, but—I like her brown eyes," Lacey Jane said. "I want to hear the song."

Miss Odenia dropped the needle on the spinning record. Instantly, a chorus of swirly violins poured into the room and then a powerful voice filled every molecule of space.

"Sweeeeeeeeeet dreeeeams of yoooouuu." The voice slipped into my body, slid down my arms and legs. It gave me the chills. I'd never heard anything like it.

If Lacey Jane could dance to Patsy Cline's song, she would win the talent part of the pageant. I could recite the entire encyclopedia, but it would be a waste of time.

"How does the song make you feel?" Miss Odenia asked her. "Let the music flow through you and move."

Lacey Jane swayed a little. She shuffled her feet to the left and then the right and did a little hop-thing. Her arms hung stiffly at her sides. Then she stopped.

She couldn't dance. Not a single step. Probably had to do with that lurching walk of hers. My heart soared. I still had a chance!

Lacey Jane burst into tears.

"Oh, honey, it's not that bad," Miss Odenia said, patting her on the back. "We'll find something else for you to do."

"No! I'm gonna dance to that song!" Lacey Jane's wet face was splotched and red. "I'll practice night and day and it'll be good! You wait!"

"All right," Miss Odenia said. "We've worked enough this morning. Let's have some refreshments. I have soft drinks and cookies left from yesterday."

When we were sitting around the kitchen table, Miss Odenia tactfully kept the conversation away from the subject of pageant talents.

"I don't think it's going to be as hot today," she said. "The paper called for only in the mid-nineties."

"Oh, yeah," I said. "Ninety-five is so much cooler than

ninety-eight. We'd better dig out our winter coats."

Miss Odenia laughed. "I had the strangest dream last night." She gazed out the window over the sink. "I was back home in Terrapin Thicket. And everything was just like it was when I was a girl. The bachelor buttons Mama grew along the fence. Our dog, Daisy, dozing under the chinaberry tree."

Personally, I get bored listening to other people's dreams because they sound so dumb. But Lacey Jane seemed to be hanging on every word.

"I walked up the porch steps," Miss Odenia went on. "And my old shoe box of paper dolls was sitting by the porch swing, where I kept it. Mama's old sewing scissors were lying there, like I'd been cutting up the Sears, Roebuck catalog and gone inside the house for a minute. I could hear Mama in the kitchen, humming as she dried dishes. In the garden, I saw a cloud of dust—Pap plowing under the cucumber patch. Oh, they both passed so many years ago, my heart squeezed to think they were alive again."

Her long slim fingers sketched her dream in the air, like watching a flower blossoming.

"And then I saw, sitting on the arm of the porch swing, my bottle of Revlon nail polish."

"Cherries in the Snow," I said.

"Yes! And don't you know I sat right down on the porch floor and pulled off my shoes and started painting my toenails. Except my feet were old and wrinkly like they are now. I was my regular old self, but inside I felt eleven or twelve again."

"What happened?" Lacey Jane asked.

"I was painting the little pinky toenail—the one that's so hard to reach—when somebody came up the walk. I could only see old work boots. I kept trying to raise my head up to see who it was, but everything above the shoes was dark, like somebody had taped my eyes partway shut. And then I woke up."

"Do you think it was Ercel?" Lacey Jane said. "Bringing you the Marriage Turtle?"

"The Marriage Turtle," I said scornfully. "Honestly, Lacey Jane, I bet you still believe in the Easter Bunny."

"Job? I don't know," Miss Odenia replied. "If it was Ercel, wouldn't I have been able to see him? Oh!—today is Saturday."

"Did you forget to set your trash out or something?" I asked.

"No, it's about telling your night-before dream on a Saturday." She thought a moment. "'Friday night's dream on the Saturday told is sure to come true, be it never so old.' I haven't remembered that in years! My granny taught me that saying."

"You don't believe that, do you?" I said. "It's not very scientific."

"Not everything has to be scientific," Lacey Jane said.

"There's some stuff you can't explain."

Miss Odenia put our glasses on the counter. "Lands, I was supposed to be at Viola's twenty minutes ago to pick up my Madame Queen order." Leaning against the sink, she toyed with the dishrag. "I'm so tired of jewelry parties and playing cards."

"Then quit," I said. Honestly, grown-ups made things so complicated. "Thanks for the Cokes. And the lesson."

Lacey Jane paused by the front door. "Did you see your mother in the dream?" she asked Miss Odenia.

She shook her head. "No, but I knew she was there."

All the way back to our trailers, Lacey Jane was quiet. But that didn't matter. I talked enough for both of us.

"Hand me that bobby pin and don't open it with your teeth," Lynette said to me. She twisted a hank of Rudy's fine bangs into a flat snail and anchored it with two criss-crossed bobby pins. "There! Pin curls with ends outside the curl. And pin curls with the ends *inside* the curl."

Rudy grinned at himself in Lynette's makeup mirror. "Cool! Metal Head!"

I wondered what Mud Hog Chuck would say if he walked in and saw his only son sprouting pin curls. No worries there. Chuck only seemed to call Lynette after Rudy was in bed. Rudy always got upset when he found out he'd missed talking to his father.

"How come you have to do such old-fashioned

hairstyles?" I asked, glancing at her cosmetology book. "Nobody wears their hair like that anymore."

"Some old lady might and I have to be able to do it." Lynette accidentally jabbed a bobby pin in Rudy's scalp. "Oops. Sorry, dipsy doodle."

The doorbell rang.

"Leave that mongrel out there," Lynette said. "Doublewide threw up on my bedspread this morning."

"Y'all home?" Lacey Jane called. I let her in. She was grinning with excitement. "Guess what? Daddy gave me thirty dollars to buy a pageant dress!"

"Well, I hope you find something real pretty," I said with fake heartiness. Lacey Jane already had a zillion dresses. Like she needed another one.

She punched me on the arm. "*Both* of us! We split the money."

"Your father's buying Rebel a pageant dress?" Lynette asked.

"Yeah. Because he's glad she's here, he said."

I looked down at the floor. Lacey Jane's father probably meant he was glad I was Lacey Jane's friend. He didn't know I was her fake friend, just like Ainsley Carter was my fake friend. She dumped me in fourth grade, but I still pretended we were best friends so I wouldn't seem so pathetic.

"Well, that's real nice of him," Lynette said. "Tell your daddy I said thanks. I'll fix a meat loaf and send it over."

As soon as me and Lacey Jane hit the hot pavement, I said, "Don't let your daddy eat Lynette's meat loaf. Not if you don't want to hear him moaning and groaning all night. Where are we gonna buy dresses for fifteen bucks?"

"Where all the trendy people shop," Lacey Jane answered. "Better-Off-Dead Pest Control and Bridal Consignment."

"We can't wear a wedding dress in a beauty pageant!"

"They have *other* dresses. For girls our age. Didn't you notice? Mrs. Randolph will help us."

She was right. The tiny old lady showed us the junior bridesmaid section.

"Most young girls wear simple tea-length dresses in summer weddings," she said. "Perfect for the pageant. You girls are so sensible. These dresses have only been worn once, and they are very reasonable."

We pawed through the racks. I was looking for something that said, "Desperate-Paleontologist-Must-Win-to-Get-to-Ice-Age-Dig." I wasn't sure what dress would look like that. Maybe brown trimmed with old bones?

Suddenly Lacey Jane gasped. She pulled out a poufy pink cupcake of a dress with puffed sleeves and a sash tied in a great big bow at the waist. Fake roses decorated the bottom of the full skirt.

It was the ugliest dress I'd ever seen in my life.

"Oh, Rebel, isn't it beautiful? I'm going to try it on." She ran to the fitting room.

There were no brown bone-trimmed dresses, but I found a turquoise dress with no sleeves and a square neck. When I held it up, the dress seemed to float.

"What do you think?" Lacey Jane swished out in the cupcake dress. The material was so stiff, the rustling skirt seemed to march ahead of her. The bell-like skirt made her stick legs look even skinnier. And that color clashed with her reddish hair.

She did a pivot turn in front of the full-length mirror. "I look so pretty!"

She looked like a lamp shade in a clown's house. Even I could tell that the turquoise was a better color for her than that icky pink. And a simpler style wouldn't make her seem so skinny.

But I wanted the turquoise dress for myself.

"It's perfect," I told her. I'd never get to the dig if I was truthful.

She twirled, making the skirt stand out, then checked the price tag. "Thirteen-fifty!" Really, a dress that ugly should be free.

I took my twelve dollar turquoise dress to the counter. Mrs. Randolph rang up our purchases and wrapped our dresses in long plastic bags. "You girls will look lovely!"

We started back down the road toward the trailer park. Lacey Jane clutched the plastic dress bag to her chest.

With her wearing that pink monstrosity, I had a better chance at the pageant. In my head, a firm voice said, "Win!

That's what it's all about!" while a smaller voice said, "Is it?" I ordered the small voice to hush up.

"Rebel," Lacey Jane said. "This dress makes me feel like—well, like my mama is still here." She glanced at me and away again. "I guess you know about my mother."

"Yeah," I said. "Miss Odenia told me. I'm sorry. But—I don't get it about the dress."

Lacey didn't answer right away. Then she said, "I know Bambi and the girls at school make fun of me because I wear ankle socks and barrettes. When Mama got too sick to go out, she'd order me stuff. I think . . ." Deep breath. "I think she thought I was younger than I am because she bought me these babyish ankle socks and barrettes."

Her voice grew quavery. I just waited and finally she spoke again.

"It was like Christmas every time Mr. Beechley came. Mama bought me ankle socks with ruffles and frogs and bunnies and stripes. And barrettes shaped like Scottie dogs and ladybugs and sparkle flowers. After a while, I didn't have time to open the packages because Mama got worse and had to go to the hospital. She never came home."

"Lacey Jane, you don't have to—"

"Let me finish. After Mama died, I found the packages. I decided I'd wear the socks and barrettes every single day because—because it made me feel closer to her." She stopped and I could see tears streaking her flushed cheeks.

I dug a used Kleenex out of my shorts pocket and gave it to her.

"I know I'm not pretty like Bambi or even you," she said, wiping her eyes.

"Me? You think I'm pretty?" I'd take even a backhanded compliment. Lynette had always been the pretty one in our family.

"But every night before Mama kissed me good night, she told me I was her pretty little girl. And this dress makes me feel like I'm Mama's pretty little girl again."

No wonder Lacey Jane had hung on to every syllable when Miss Odenia told her dream. I bet Lacey Jane wanted to dream that her mother was back, too.

For once in my life, I couldn't think of a single thing to say. We walked in silence down the heat-shimmered road, our plastic dress bags sticking to our sweaty bare legs.

From the Field Notebook of Rebel McKenzie

Once upon a time there was a poor paleontologist girl. She didn't have any money to go on digs so she went to work for her evil older sister in the hottest trailer park kingdom in Virginia.

Every day Paleontella would fix special meals for picky Prince Rudy. She made beds and swept floors and washed dirty underpants and scrubbed pots and pans and fed the pet Andrewsarchus. She rearranged the gravel in the driveway and polished the whole trailer with toilet paper. And every day her evil older sister went out into the world to learn how to be beautiful. (Only it wasn't working.)

One day Paleontella was so tired she sat down and cried. All of a sudden her Fairy Mastodon appeared!

"I will grant you one wish," her Fairy Mastodon said.

"Oh! I'd love to go on a dig!" said Paleontella. "But my evil older sister gives me too much work."

"Well, she's not around, is she?" The Fairy Mastodon waved her magic tusk and said, "Go! But be back before sundown."

"What will happen if I don't?" Paleontella asked fearfully.

"Your evil older sister will come home from learning how to be beautiful and beat the crap out of you."

"I'll be back! Thank you, Fairy Mastodon! You've made me the happiest poor paleontologist girl in the whole trailer park kingdom!"

ELEVEN

Lunch with God

"Rebel, take out the garbage," Lynette said. "It smells to high heaven."

"Rudy," I said. "Take out the garbage."

"I asked you," Lynette said.

"Isn't it time he had some responsibility?"

Lynette took her nose out of her textbook and looked at Rudy, who was racing his cars along the kitchen floor. "Baby, would you be a pumpkin pie and take out the garbage?"

"No," Rudy said, skimming two cars over the coffee table. "There's always flies around the trash cans. And I'm scared of flies."

I hooted. "Nobody is scared of flies!"

"I am. They look at me with mean red eyes. I'll go if Rebel comes with me."

I heaved out of my comfy chair and grabbed the paper bag. "All right. Or do you want to put on a suit of armor first?"

He stuffed cars in his pockets. "It's not funny."

We went outside and walked over to the big trash cans. Flies formed big black clots on mounds of steaming garbage. They flew up in a swarm as we approached.

I gave the bag to Rudy. "Here. Throw it in."

He screeched and dropped the bag. "They're looking at me with their red eyes!"

Now I had to pick up loose trash. When I was done, Rudy said, "Will you play cars with me? Pleeease?"

This was one of those evenings Rudy was going to worry me to pieces. I put up with him all day and needed a little quiet. "Your daddy's supposed to call tonight."

"He is?"

"Yeah, but it'll be late because of the time difference. You need to get some sleep before he calls." Well, Chuck *could* call tonight and ask to speak to Rudy.

Rudy beat me back to the trailer and was in bed before the flies had settled back on the garbage.

I woke with a jerk and listened to the fan whirring in the darkness. I had the creepy feeling not that somebody was in the room but that somebody *wasn't*. Leaning over, I switched on the nightstand lamp.

Rudy's bed was empty.

He never got up for a drink of water or to go to the bathroom. Once his head hit the pillow, that kid was dead to the world.

This could only mean one thing: Rudy was sleepwalking.

I went to the door, my heart thumping. I had to find him. But what if I did and he got all crazy or something? Lynette warned me not to wake him up.

I tiptoed into the kitchen. The clock over the fridge read one thirty-five. A dark lump on the back of the sofa stirred slightly. Doublewide. Where was Rudy? I crept through the living room and down the hall to Lynette's room.

Lynette was sprawled on her back in the water bed, snoring like a band saw. No Rudy. I checked the bathroom, even behind the shower curtain. Not there either.

Where is that kid?

What if he'd slipped outside? Lynette would kill me if anything happened to her Rudy while I was sleeping in the same room. I'd feel pretty crummy myself.

I unlocked the front door and ran down the steps. Something squished under my bare foot. In the streetlamp, I saw thick black shapes on the front steps. *Slugs*.

I hopped back inside and wiped my slimy foot on the mat. Then I hurried into Lynette's room and snapped on the light.

"Wha—?" She sat up, her face dotted with Noxzema.

"Rudy's gone!" I said. "I've looked all over. I think he sleepwalked outside!"

She was up in a flash, shoving her feet into flip-flops. I found another pair of flip-flops and slipped them on. We flew out the door.

A damp haze—heat left over from the day—hung over the trailer park. We ran down the street. I spotted a small figure lit by an orange cone of light heading for the sewer pipe.

Lynette reached him first. "Rudy," she said, gently taking his arm.

His cowlicky hair stood up like a rooster's tail. "Did we give Mud Hog a bath?"

"What?" I said. Then I remembered Lynette saying sleepwalkers seem like they're awake. They talk and everything.

"Yes," Lynette told him. "Mud Hog is nice and clean. Let's go home, okay?"

"We'll win the next one." His voice sounded thin and hopeful, but his eyes were vacant.

I took his other arm. "C'mon, Rude. Time to get ready for the next race."

"Okay." He let us lead him back to our trailer, quiet as a lamb. Lynette tucked him in, and he closed his eyes. We waited to make sure he was asleep for real.

Then we went out to the kitchen. Lynette fixed a pot of coffee. It tasted horrible, but I drank it anyway.

"Rudy hasn't sleepwalked like this in a long time," she told me. "Usually it's because he's upset over something."

Like thinking his father is going to call and he doesn't? I gulped the scalding coffee and choked.

She set her cup down with a clink. "What did you do to him, Rebel?"

I fessed up because Lynette would wring the truth out of me anyway. "I didn't mean to make him sleepwalk. I just wanted him to give it a rest, you know, wanting to play and talk and all."

"He's a little boy," she said angrily. "You don't put him on a shelf till you're ready to take him down again. You'll find that out when you have kids of your own."

"I'm not having kids," I said. "I'm never getting married. I'm going to be a paleontologist, and that's it."

"Well, I hope you and your skeletons will be very happy. It's a shame you don't want to spend more time with your nephew. He thinks the sun rises and sets in you." She picked up our cups and rinsed them in the sink. "Let's go to bed, Rebel."

I dropped into my canoe-bed and thought about what my sister said. Nobody had ever liked me that much before (not counting my parents). Certainly not Ainsley Carter, who never gave me the time of day at school.

The next thing I knew, Lynette was yelling at me to get up. I staggered into the kitchen.

"I'm in a big ol' rush," she said. "Be good to Rudy today, okay? And will you tidy up the bathroom?"

Tidy! Lynette left enough hair in the bathroom sink to

knit a whole other sister. I griped while I flushed the yucky stuff down the drain. Then I hung up her wet towels—three of them! She only has one body. Why does she need three towels?

Because Lynette tore out in "a big ol' rush," I had to make her sloshy water bed (but not too neat) and wipe spilled makeup off her dresser (with her best skirt that was lying on the floor). Then I realized she was late because she hadn't had much sleep. And whose fault was that?

Rudy was sitting on a sofa cushion in front of the TV watching cartoons when I finally finished. "Rebel, I'm hungry," he said.

"Want a bowl of Lucky Charms?"

"No."

"How about an RC float?"

"No."

I folded my arms across my chest. "Well, what *do* you want?"

He clutched the cushion to his stomach and whined, "I don't know."

I felt annoyed until I remembered what he'd said last night. *Did we give Mud Hog a bath?* How sad was that?

"All right, I'll fix you something special." French toast was my favorite not-feeling-so-hot breakfast, but I didn't know how to make it.

I put two slices of Wonder bread in the toaster. Next I melted a little margarine in a skillet and added a dollop of

Karo syrup. I let the toast sizzle in the syrup mixture on both sides. Then I put the fried syrup-bread on a plate and cut the squares into triangles to make them fancy.

"Here you are. A breakfast invented just for you—Rudy Cakes. Delicioso!"

Rudy dug in. "Rebel, you're a good cook!"

I fed Doublewide before he passed out from hunger, washed the sticky skillet and dishes, wiped down the counters and stove, and was making our beds when Rudy came in and asked, "What're we gonna do today?"

"Haven't thought about it."

Lacey Jane had gone someplace with her father, and we didn't have another pageant lesson until tomorrow. I could practice my talent, but I didn't like any of Henry Wadsworth Longfellow's poems.

"Know what?" Rudy said, fiddling with the cap on my canteen.

"What?" I tugged the sheet over the hole in my bed.

"That's what. Know what?"

"*What?*"

"That's what." He giggled. "Know—"

I grabbed his bony wrist. "You know what? You're gonna be extinct if you don't knock it off."

"Let's go fossil hunting today!" He took my geologist's hammer from my backpack and tapped Tusky's knee like a doctor testing reflexes. "Can we, Rebel? Huh, can we? Can we, huh?"

"Where can we look for fossils around here?" The ancient couple in the trailer at the end of the street didn't count.

"Down by the sewer pipe! There's a ton of rocks and stuff in the field!"

Normally, spending a hot day next to an open sewer line would not exactly thrill me. But I then realized something. When the construction guys put in the sewer, they had probably dug pretty deep. Dirt and rocks that hadn't been disturbed for thousands of years were now on top of that vacant lot.

"Rudy, fill this canteen with Kool-Aid. We're going fossil hunting."

All the way down to the vacant lot, he scampered in front of me like a puppy, running backward to say, "I had a good idea, didn't I, Rebel? The best idea of anyone. Right?"

And all the way down to the vacant lot, I had to agree he had a good idea. I was glad Rudy hadn't invented electricity, or I would have to tell him how great he was every time I cut the light on.

The gassy smell from the sewer pipe nearly knocked me over.

"Pee-yew!" I set my backpack on the ground, wishing I had brought a clothespin for my nose. "How do you stand to play down here?"

"You get used to it. See that bunch of rocks over there?

That's where the good fossils are."

I pinched my nostrils shut. "Oh, for heaven's sake, Rudy," I said, my voice all nasal. "Fossils don't hang out like people at a cocktail party. You look for clues."

"What kind of clues?"

"Look for rocks that are real smooth or have a pattern. Those could be ammonites—creatures that lived in the sea. A long, long time ago, this whole area was covered by the ocean." I liked telling my nephew about fossils. Maybe he'd be a paleontologist like me.

"I found a tooth!" He held up a small object.

"Rudy, that's from a plastic comb. Fossils aren't made of plastic," I said. "Anyway, my book says it's hard to find a whole fossil or even a tooth. Most of the time you find pieces of them."

"Hey, a turtle!" A turtle with yellow spots on its dark brown shell lumbered toward a puddle. The turtle lifted his beaky nose when Rudy ran over.

"Don't stick your finger in his face," I said. "He'll bite."

"I just want to look at him. He's kind of cute." The turtle had the good sense to amble away.

"Quit zooming all over the place," I told Rudy. "Paleontologists don't run like people in an earthquake. You search a small area at a time."

He beamed at me. "I like it when you talk fossil stuff, Rebel. You're so smart. I want to be like you."

Every rotten thought I ever had about the kid flew

out the window. If I got him interested in paleontology, maybe he wouldn't be such a pain. But I felt a twinge, too. A few weeks ago Rudy had wanted to be just like his daddy and drive monster trucks. What would Rudy do when I left for the August Kids' Dig?

I staked out a small section as far from the sewer pipe as possible. Broken rocks were scattered in clay baked so hard, weeds couldn't even grow. Me and Rudy squatted in the heat, turning over rocks and sifting pebbles. Even though I wore a T-shirt, my back felt like it was on fire.

"Rebel!" Rudy shrieked after a while. "Look!"

With his luck, I figured it was a bedspring or something, but, no, the little stinker had dug up a smooth solid black rock chipped around the edges like a piecrust.

"Is it a fossil?" he asked, thumbing his glasses up on his nose.

I examined the rock through my magnifying glass. "It's an arrowhead, Rude. See these marks here? They could have been made with a tool. The rock is obsidian."

"I found a narrowhead!" When he tried to take it back, I held on to the arrowhead a little too long. Leave it to that kid to make a real discovery.

"It's hotter'n thunder out here," I said. "Let's go back."

"I can't wait to show Mama my narrowhead!"

"If you do, she'll know we were down by the sewer pipe and we'll get in trouble."

"Oh."

By the time we straggled back to our trailer, it was lunchtime, and Lacey Jane Whistle was sitting on our porch steps. Today she had on green shorts and a white top with frogs. It goes without saying what decorated her ankle socks and barrettes.

"Where've you been?" she asked.

"Fossil hunting," I said.

"I saw a turtle! And I found a real Indian narrowhead!" Rudy cried, pulling it from his pocket. "See?"

"You're a Narrow Head, all right. Your fingernails are filthy," Lacey Jane remarked. "What did *you* find, Rebel?"

"Where have you been?" I asked her instead. I didn't want her to know a seven-year-old had showed me up.

Her mouth drew a line like it did when she didn't want to answer. "Daddy had an appointment this morning. I went with him, and then we went to the cemetery. I put pink roses on Mama's grave. They were her favorite."

Rudy stared at her. I was so afraid he was going to ask Lacey Jane what color dress her mother was laid out in and how many cars drove to the graveside service.

But he simply said, "I bet your mama can see those roses and thinks they're real pretty."

Lacey Jane gave him a weak smile.

"I'm starving," I said, flinging open the trailer door. "Let's eat lunch. And Rudy, whatever I fix, you're going to eat, you hear?"

157

I made us open-faced peanut-butter-and-potato-chip sandwiches. My cooking skills were growing by leaps and bounds.

"Rudy, take three RCs out of the fridge and set them on the table. And get the bag of animal crackers."

"I don't want to eat inside," he said in that whiny tone that made my jaw clench. "I always eat outside, 'member? Lacey Jane, will you eat outside with me?"

"Lacey Jane doesn't want to bake on the front steps. Take your stuff and go out."

"I'll eat with you," Lacey Jane told him, picking up her plate.

That left me and Doublewide. We went outside, too.

"Isn't this cozy?" I said sarcastically. The three of us, plus one large fuzzy cat, were packed together on the top step, balancing plates on our slick knees. "I think I'll get us a blanket so we won't catch a chill."

"Oh, stop," said Lacey Jane. "It's not that bad."

Tilting my head back, I pulled on my RC. Then I let rip an enormous belch. "Ahhh. Better."

"You are so gross." But Lacey Jane grinned.

"Rebel, you said you were going to learn me how to burp-talk like that," Rudy said. "Will you learn me now?"

"Teach, not learn. Okay, first you have to control your breath. Can you hold your breath at least a minute? I'll time you. Go!"

Rudy sucked in a giant breath, clamped his mouth

shut, and puffed his cheeks out like a squirrel in a barrel of peanuts.

"You don't even have a watch," Lacey Jane said.

"I'm counting in my head."

Rudy looked at me, his eyes bulging.

"Not yet. Almost—"

He let his breath out in a shuddering gasp. "How'd I do?"

"Fourteen seconds. You need to work on it. When you take a bath tonight, hold your head under the water for a really long time."

"I'll go under a whole hour!"

"Okay, next you have to drink a big swallow of a fizzy drink. Like this." I slugged back half my RC.

"I'm moving out of range," Lacey Jane said, scuttling to the ground.

"Me, too!" Rudy scampered down the steps.

Cowards. I waited until I felt like a rocket was going off in my stomach, then I opened my mouth and out came a long, magnificent belch. When it was over, I said, "At least a forty-five-seconder."

Lacey Jane sat down next to me again, but Rudy had a strange expression on his face.

"You gotta move over," he said, a little desperately. "He's here."

"Who's here?" I asked, looking around.

"God. We have to leave a space for Him." He perched

on the very end of the step, leaving a gap between him and Lacey Jane.

She nudged me. "*What* is he talking about?"

"He has lunch with God," I whispered. "Lynette thinks it's a phase, but if you ask me—"

"You're kidding." Lacey Jane turned to Rudy. "How do you know He's here?"

"See that cloud?" Rudy pointed at a puffy cloud over the fire station. "That's God's house."

"God lives in a cloud?" I said.

"Where else? He owns the whole *sky*." He looked at me like I was a mental case. "Last year, when I was just a little kid, I saw God in a cloud like that one. I think He likes to come down and visit, you know?"

"But how come He only visits you?" asked Lacey Jane.

He shrugged. "When I saw the God-cloud, I wrote Him a letter asking for stuff."

"Like Santa Claus?" Trying to keep up with Rudy's logic was impossible.

"No, like *God*."

I twirled a leaf in front of Doublewide's nose. "What'd you ask for?"

"I wanted a truck that runs with this radio thing. And I wanted Mud Hog to win a race." Propping his elbows on his knees, he dropped his chin on his fists. "But mostly I asked for Daddy to be home more."

Lacey Jane studied the empty space between them. She

started to stick her hand out, then pulled it back.

"Do you think He knows I'm here?" she asked seriously.

"Definitely. But I'm not sure about Rebel."

Personally, I thought we'd humored him long enough about this lunch-with-God business.

"Rudy," I said, "would God like an RC? Or an animal cracker? How about a napkin?" I couldn't imagine that God would be a sloppy eater, but maybe He wanted to be treated like everybody else.

"Rebel, be still," Lacey Jane ordered. "You're such an attention hog."

"Am not."

Put out, I petted Doublewide, who lay between my bare feet. The cat twisted his head away, his red rhinestone collar winking in the bright sun. Doublewide's blue eyes were wide and staring, as if he could see something I couldn't.

From the Field Notebook of Rebel McKenzie

Rudy was reading my *How and Why Wonder Book of Prehistoric Mammals*. Part of the book is about dinosaurs and early fish and stuff. Rudy was looking at a picture of a *Stupendemys geographicus*, a long-necked turtle eight feet long.

He asked me to read about turtles. Prehistoric turtles lived 220 million years ago! Today's turtles look like the ancient ones. Box turtles are common. Rudy found one today. The turtle Miss Odenia's friend painted with fingernail polish was that kind. They have hinged shells so they can pull their head inside and close it like a box.

They live 40 to 70 years. Some of them live to be 100! You can tell their age by the rings on their shells, but only up to 15 years. Box turtles can travel 130 miles in a single day! So much for thinking turtles are slow. They won't stay in a new place, but walk to get back home.

Rudy was very interested. Maybe he'll be a paleontologist after all. Anything would be better than planning people's funerals.

TWELVE

The Great Wiglet Escapade

The pageant was four days away. Lacey Jane and me were discussing what shoes to wear with our dresses as we walked to Miss Odenia's for talent practice.

"Mama took me to the doctor this morning," I said, shifting the two books I carried. "And he said my heels were almost better. But I still can't wear closed-back shoes. I can't wear these ol' rubber flip-flops with a beauty contest dress!"

Lacey Jane lined her foot up with mine. "We're about the same size. I have some white sandals that would look good with your dress. They don't have a strap across the back."

"Thanks. What're you gonna do with your hair?"

"Maybe put it up," Lacey Jane said. "I guess your sister will do yours."

"I haven't asked her." Truth was, I didn't want Lynette

teasing my hair into a haystack. This morning when she had left for beauty school, Lynette's hair was kicked up like a pig had been rooting for acorns in it.

"What's that other book?" Lacey Jane asked. "I know the one Miss Odenia let you borrow."

"The poem one, yeah. I'm using my favorite book. It's way better than poetry."

Lacey Jane said urgently, "There's Bambi. Make like you don't see her."

Playing like you don't see Bambi Lovering is like trying to ignore a brass band.

"Woo-hoo!" she called. "Rebel! Lacey Jane! I got something to show you."

"If she yammers more than three minutes," I said in a low voice, "I'll act like I'm having a heart attack, and you say you have to go dial 911."

Bambi rushed up, Kissy cradled in her arm. The little Yorkie's topknot was looped with a blue bow and her tiny pink tongue hung out like a postage stamp. Bambi set Kissy on the ground and let the dog run around in circles.

"I just got back from the photographer's," Bambi said, brandishing a cardboard folder, which she opened. Inside were huge full-color photographs of Bambi in a glittery red shirt holding Kissy (who had a matching red hair bow). They were posed in front of a filmy white curtain.

"So?" I said. "Big deal."

"These are head shots," Bambi said in an overly

important tone. "Professional pictures for my portfolio. Pick them up by the edges so you don't smudge them."

"I can see fine from here," I said, making no move to touch Bambi's stupid pictures.

"Mama says I should be in commercials. I'm not crazy about the idea, but I figure with all the money I'll make, I can start my beauty empire even faster."

"Lacey Jane," I said, gazing up at the sky, "do you hear anything?"

"Just some boring ol' droning sound."

"Must be a big mosquito," I said.

Bambi pouted. "Very funny. Mama's going to send these shots to a dog food company. She says me and Kissy are a natural to advertise dog food."

"Makes sense," I said, "since you both eat dog chow." Lacey Jane snorted with laughter.

Bambi slammed the cardboard folder shut and snatched up Kissy in mid-circle. "You think you're so smart, Rebel McKenzie. You don't stand a chance at the pageant so you might as well drop out now. You too, Lacey Jane."

"And miss beating the pants off you?" Lacey Jane said. "I don't think so."

"Don't bother clearing a spot for that trophy!" I yelled after Bambi.

"I already have," she flung back, walking so fast Kissy's little head joggled up and down like a cork in rough water.

* * *

I had to knock a bunch of times before Miss Odenia finally opened her door.

"Sorry, girls," she said. "I was cleaning out my closet. C'mon in."

"We can come back, if you want," Lacey Jane said.

"No, no. The pageant is Friday. You need to work on your talent. Tomorrow we'll practice the interview and the next day we'll have a dress rehearsal, walking, talent, all of it. So bring your outfits."

I laid *Complete American Poems* on her dining room table.

"Which poem did you choose?" Miss Odenia asked.

"None." I held up the *How and Why Wonder Book of Prehistoric Mammals*. "I made up my own story. From this."

"But that's a science book," Miss Odenia said. "Won't it be hard to turn it into a dramatic reading?"

I waved them toward the sofa. "Sit down and prepare to be amazed." I turned my back on them and waited a few seconds. Then I began speaking quietly.

"Forty thousand years ago, the land in one spot in Los Angeles was different than it is now. Oil seeped from the ground. It was the end of a time period called the Pleistocene epoch. During this time, the earth was in the grip of the Great Ice Age!"

I whirled around to face the audience and whispered.

"It is morning at the La Brea tar pits. A thirsty quagga wanders down to the pool to get a drink. The heavy creature picks its way through fallen leaves to find the water." I tiptoed exaggeratedly, like I was on stilts. My voice got louder.

167

"Its heavy hooves get stuck in the asphalt hidden beneath the leaves. Trapped, the quagga screamed!"

I let out a high-pitched yelp. *"Rarff!"* Miss Odenia started.

"Unable to move, the terrified animal shrieked and struggled to get free." I threw myself on the floor. Keeping my legs still, I flailed my arms. *"The quagga's cries let a saber-toothed lion (really, a Smilodon) know it was in trouble."*

I hopped up again and stuck two fingers on either side of my mouth, like curved sabers. *"The big cat wades into the tar pit, eager for its easy meal. The cat rips the quagga's belly open with its huge teeth."*

I pretended to tear open the quagga's belly. Then I stopped, a look of pure terror on my face (I'd practiced in the bathroom mirror).

"The cat's paws get stuck too! Mired in the tar, the big cat snarls, attracting other, bigger predators. Meat-eating birds swoop down"— I flapped my arms—*"and land on the dying animals. But their feathers dip into the tar and they are trapped, too. Soon all the animals lay in the pit. Dead forever."*

I ended by lying twisted on the floor, my eyes wide with horror as I stared sightlessly up at the ceiling.

Lacey Jane clapped, and finally Miss Odenia joined her.

"What'd you think?" I said, getting up.

"It's an *unusual* piece," Miss Odenia remarked. "But . . . maybe you shouldn't do quite so much acting?"

"That's the best part," I said. "I'm going to work on it

some more and act out every sentence. Maybe every *word*!"

Miss Odenia rose to put the Patsy Cline album on her record player. "Well. Okay, Lacey Jane. Your turn."

She didn't budge. "I can't go after a terrific act like Rebel's."

"It wasn't that good, really," I said modestly, though I knew it was a showstopper.

"You can't be shy," Miss Odenia told her. "Everyone will be watching you at the pageant. Maybe do one run-through for us? So you won't get stage fright?"

Lacey Jane shook her head. "I want my talent to be a surprise."

It'll be a surprise all right, I thought, if she did that awful dance. At least Lacey Jane wouldn't be any competition in the talent part of the pageant. I only had to worry about Bambi. I didn't know the other girls who'd entered, but they were probably no threat.

Miss Odenia always gave us cold drinks after our lesson, but she just sat there looking a little bit like a tar-stuck quagga herself.

I cleared my throat. "All that reciting made me awful thirsty."

"I don't know where my mind is this morning. Or my manners," Miss Odenia said, going into the kitchen. "How about some Hawaiian Punch?"

While she poured our drinks, I noticed an envelope propped against a Thom McAn shoe box on the kitchen table. Using my special ability to read upside down, I saw the return address.

Terrapin Thicket.

"Hey," I said. "Did you get a letter from that guy? What's his name?"

"Ercel Grady. I certainly did," she replied. "I've been up half the night fretting over that letter."

"How come?" Lacey Jane asked.

"He wants me to go down for a visit."

"So, go," I said.

"I'm not sure I want to. A lot of water has passed under the bridge since I saw Ercel last." Miss Odenia flipped the lid of the shoe box, revealing a bunch of old letters, post-cards, and photographs.

I picked out a bottle of dried-up nail polish. Cherries in the Snow. "You kept all this stuff."

"Yes." She sighed. "Even if I want to go, I don't have the money for a bus ticket."

"Maybe he can pay your way," Lacey Jane suggested.

Miss Odenia gave a weak smile. "Ercel thinks I'm a famous hand model still. He'd be shocked to find out my fixed income barely pays my monthly bills."

The answer seemed simple to me. "Tell him to come up here. You want to see him, don't you?"

She studied her hands. They were smooth, with long fingers and nails like flower petals. "I do and I don't. It's hard to explain. When you're older you'll understand."

Why did grown-ups always pull that "when you're older" bit? It was clear to me that Miss Odenia was mixed up in her own mind but she didn't want to admit it.

Lacey Jane looked at her own hands. Her fingers were long like Miss Odenia's, but she chewed her nails.

"Maybe," she said, "you'll figure out that dream you had. And then you'll know what to do."

Miss Odenia nodded. "You might be right, Lacey Jane. Maybe the answer to my problem is in that dream."

I didn't put much stock in dreams. Nosiree, cold hard cash was the answer to *my* problem.

"Mama brung me a live white mouse!" Rudy exclaimed, practically foaming at the mouth.

Lynette came in from work, juggling her tote bag, purse, and a fake woman's head with a fringe of white hair pinned to it. She set the head down on the kitchen table. "This is not a mouse, Rudy. It's a wiglet."

"What's that?" I asked. "A wig for a bald-headed baby?" I broke myself up.

"It's a hairpiece you stick on the back of your head," she explained. "To fill in where you don't have much hair. Maxie, one of the girls at Hair Magic, gave it to me to work on. Her best customer is going to a wedding and wants it styled."

I unpinned the wiglet and held it on the back of my hand. "'Hi, everybody! I'm Mr. Peepers!" I balled my hand into a fist and moved my thumb like a mouth.

Doublewide jumped up on the chair next to me and cocked his head. I was pretty good at this. Even the cat was entertained. Maybe I should do a puppet act for my talent.

Rudy giggled. "Hi, Mr. Peepers."

"Good-bye, Mr. Peepers." Lynette grabbed the wiglet away from me. "I have to fix this tonight and give it to Maxie. I'm being paid and everything. My first real hair assignment!"

"Not counting the chain saw haircut."

"Ha-ha. When I get done, and *if* everybody is good, we'll go for a Slurpee run."

All of us, even Doublewide, watched Lynette shampoo the wiglet in the sink. Then she blow-dried it partway and used her hot rollers. After pinning it back on the fake head, she teased big fat curls into swirls, tucking the ends in with the rat tail of her comb.

"It looks like a fancy cake," Rudy remarked, as Lynette blasted her creation with hair spray.

"It *does* look like icing on a wedding cake. My Rudy-peepers is so smart!"

"Can we go get Slurpees now?" I asked.

Lynette placed the mannequin head on the top of the fridge and gathered up her purse and car keys. We piled into The Clunker and zipped down the dusty road to the 7-Eleven. Besides the Slurpees, Lynette bought me a roll of Necco Wafers and Rudy a cherry Tootsie Pop.

"What did the doctor say?" she asked me on the way back home. "Today was your appointment, wasn't it?"

"My heels are almost better. And get this! Mama and Daddy are going to Ocean City for two weeks!" No wonder they were so eager to get rid of me. They stuffed me in a hot trailer park so they could go to the beach.

"Oh, for heaven's sake," said Lynette, pulling into our driveway. "Mama and Daddy haven't been away in years. But that means they won't be at the pageant."

I was glad. The fewer witnesses seeing me sprint to cash the check and hop a bus to Saltville, the better.

Savoring my Slurpee, I was last to get out of the car. When I heard my sister scream like a herd of quaggas trapped in a tar pit, I hurried inside.

In the kitchen, my sister stood in shock. The mannequin head lay tumbled on the floor, a few pearl-topped pins still stabbed in it.

The wiglet was missing.

"*Where is it?*" she screeched. "It was *right there* when we left! Who stole my wiglet?"

Doublewide crouched under the kitchen table, washing one of his front paws. He quit licking when he realized we were all staring at him. Guilt flickered in his crossed eyes.

Lynette dove under the kitchen table, but the cat fled into the living room.

"*That CAT!*" She hollered so loud, the dishes in the

drainer rattled. *"I'm going to KILL him!"*

Just as she lunged for him, Doublewide streaked behind the sofa. "Block the other end!" she yelled, shoving an end table aside to crouch by the opening.

"Lynette," I said. "Do you think the cat is going to *tell* you what he did with that wiglet? He's so scared he'll probably tee-tee on the floor."

"You're right." She struggled to her feet. "Fan out and look in all Doublewide's favorite hiding places. The wiglet has to be here somewhere."

I checked Rudy's room, peering under the beds, underneath Tusky, in the closet. No wiglet. I helped Lynette go through her bedroom. She ripped the covers off her water bed, tossed the pillows on the floor, and picked up the clothes she always left on her floor. I pitched every shoe out of her closet.

No wiglet.

Rudy stood on the kitchen counter, taking boxes of cereal and macaroni and spaghetti from the cabinets.

"Doublewide can't open cupboards," I told him.

"Yes, he can. He opens the bottom one all the time. I seen him. He sits up and pulls with his paw until he gets it open."

"That's because we keep the cat food down there. He can't reach the upper cabinets."

Lynette tore back into the living room. Frantically, she lobbed chair cushions into the corners and even scattered her fashion magazines off the coffee table.

"Lynette, get a grip," I said. "We'll find it. It'll probably be a little messed up—"

"It had better not be or that cat's gonna have more than a kink in his tail!"

"Okay, we have to think like Doublewide," I said. "What's his favorite, favorite place in all the world?"

We looked at each other, then said at once, "The bathroom!"

We raced to the bathroom, but it wasn't big enough for three of us to be in there at the same time. Lynette hauled out the wicker clothes basket and began flinging clothes every which way.

Rudy looked behind the shower curtain and under the bath mat and in the sink. There was only one place left.

I got down on my hands and knees and reached behind the toilet. My fingers met something wet and furry. I pulled it out.

Water dripped from a mass of slimy tangled white hair.

Lynette's eyes bulged. "Oh, my God! It's *ruined*!"

"No, it's not," I said. "Just wash it like you did before and dry it and fix curls and it'll be good as new—"

"Half the hair is gone!"

She was right about that. Doublewide had clearly had a field day with the hairpiece. But even if he'd gnawed on it for a week, he didn't have that much spit to make it so sopping wet.

I lifted the toilet seat. Strands of white hair clung to the sides of the toilet bowl. "I think he tried to wash it himself."

"He *played* with it in the toilet!" Lynette's face was so red, I thought she was having a stroke. "I'll have to *pay* for Maxie's customer's hairpiece. They won't trust me with another job till I've had my state license twenty years."

Just then, a seal-colored nose poked into the doorway. Doublewide, who had the worst timing in the universe, came to see if he was forgiven. Or maybe to claim his toy.

Lynette saw him and freaked. "You dare show your face after what you did! I'm gonna uncross your eyes!"

She chased him down the hall. I was amazed at how fast that big cat could run. His ears were flat as he covered some ground.

"No more *Wagon Train*!" Lynette hollered. "No more pudding cups!"

I had left the front door open. Doublewide dashed through it and sprang into the yard without hitting the steps. With a flash of ruby rhinestones, the cat disappeared down the street.

"Doublewide!" Rudy called, running after him. He turned to me with stricken eyes. "Doublewide's run off!"

"Don't worry," I said. "He'll be back. Have you ever known that cat to miss a meal?"

But I was wrong.

MISSING

(Runaway)

SIAMESE CAT

Answers to the name of Doublewide

(The Wonder Cat)

21 Pounds
Blue Eyes (Crossed)
Kink Tail
Dark Brown Fur

Wearing Fake Ruby Stone Collar

Likes "Wagon Train"
and Vanilla Pudding Cups

If found, call 555-8770

WARNING:

Cat may be hard to catch due to hurt feelings.

THIRTEEN

The Ten-Pound
Three-Ounce Baby

First thing next morning, Rudy hurried outside in his NASCAR pajamas and bare feet to see if Doublewide had returned. No cat sat on the patio table, paw raised to ring the doorbell.

"He's gone forever!" Rudy wailed. "He's run away from home!"

"He likes his four square meals a day too much to leave home," I said. "And you. You're his best buddy."

But when Doublewide hadn't come back by lunchtime, even I was worried.

"Mama," Rudy said, "can we drive around and look for Doublewide?"

"Honeybunch, I have a great big huge exam to study for." Lynette sat hunched at the table, surrounded by papers and charts and her cosmetology book. "When I get through studying and if he hasn't come back, we'll go. Okay? And your daddy is supposed to call this evening."

It seemed too much to hope for, but if Chuck actually called Rudy for once, the kid might not feel so bad.

"I know," I said to him. "Let's make posters. You know, in case somebody finds Doublewide. We'll put them around the trailer park."

Rudy ran to his room and came out with markers and his old school tablet. He ripped out about five hundred sheets. "I'll tell you what to say and you write it down."

After I'd made enough posters to plaster a football stadium, I asked Lynette for some tape.

"Unh," she grunted, and mumbled something about electrolysis.

I fished around in her beauty school first-aid kit for her adhesive tape. Then me and Rudy went outside.

"Let's put one on the mailbox row," I said. "Lots of people will see it there." We walked all over Grandview Estates, taping posters to street signs and light poles.

On our way back, Lacey Jane came out of her trailer. "Ready, Rebel?"

"For what?"

"Our pageant lesson. And then we're serving at Miss Odenia's card party."

I smacked my forehead. "I plumb forgot! Rudy, run on home. Tell Lynette I'm at Miz Odenia's and I'll be back in a little while. Okay?"

The card table was set up, and Miss Odenia had laid out the platters for us to use later.

"You didn't happen to see a large brown cat?" I asked. "He ran away."

"Doublewide? No, but I'll keep an eye out for him." She sat down on the sofa. The coffee table was clear except for a single pad of paper and a pen. "I've prepared three questions. They should give you an idea of what the interview is like."

"Why do we get interviewed anyway?" I asked.

"The judges base their decision on appearance, personality, and talent. Your personality should shine in the interview part." She picked up the pad. "Rebel, I'll interview you first. Stand like I taught you and smile. *Always* smile."

I placed the heel of my right foot in the arch of my left foot, clasped my hands in front, and smiled so hard, the tendons in my neck strained.

"I said smile, Rebel, not grimace. All right. Miss Rebel McKenzie is our first contestant. Rebel, tell us your life's ambition."

This was easy. "I want to be a paleontologist—the Ice Age kind, not the dinosaur kind. Oh, and I want to save the world."

"Rebel, don't stretch your lips when you talk. And do you really mean you want to save the world?"

"Yeah, why not?"

She pointed her pen. "Rule Number One, be specific.

Rule Number Two, be sincere. Judges can spot a phony like an ace-no-face in a hand of nines and tens."

"Uh—okay."

Miss Odenia sat back again. "Next question. Rebel McKenzie, if I was a stranger in your town and you gave me a tour, where would you take me first?"

My smile dropped. "Huh?"

"It sounds strange, but you never know what the judges will ask. Don't answer right away," she advised. "Always take at least three seconds to figure out what you want to say. And repeat the question back first. That gives you a little more time."

"Okay. Umm—"

"No 'um.'" She waggled her pen at me. "You want to sound confident."

"Okay, if I was—no, if *you* were a stranger in town and I gave you a tour, I'd take you to . . . Kline's Tastee Freez because they have the best twist cones in Virginia."

"Good! Last question. If someone gave you a million dollars, what would you do with it?"

A million dollars! All those zeros swam before my eyes. I'd buy Frog Level Middle School and close it so I wouldn't have to go anymore, and then I'd buy a private jet and a pilot so I could fly to any prehistoric dig I wanted, and—

"Don't keep the judges waiting too long," she reminded me.

What would the judges want to hear? I cleared my throat and said, "If someone gave me a million dollars, I'd—I'd help all the poor people. Is that good, Miss Odenia?"

"Be more specific. You know, like you'd help a family whose house has burned down or something. That way the judges will think you're sincere. Not bad, Rebel. Okay, Lacey Jane, let's see how you do."

I took her seat as she got up. "No fair. She heard the questions already and had time to think about her answers."

"The judges may ask her the same questions," Miss Odenia said. "Or they might change them. Now, Miss Lacey Jane Whistle, tell us your life's ambition."

"I want to get married and have six children," she replied, smiling. "And I also want to be either a detective, veterinarian, or ballerina."

You can cross the last one off your list, I thought. A mastodon at a tea party was more graceful than Lacey Jane.

"Very good," Miss Odenia said. "If I was a stranger in town and you gave me a tour, where would you take me first?"

Lacey Jane took exactly three seconds, then she said quietly, "If you were a stranger in town and I gave you a tour, I'd take you to the cemetery because it's the prettiest, most peaceful spot."

Miss Odenia nodded. "And last, Lacey Jane, if someone gave you a million dollars, what would you do with it?"

The smile left Lacey's Jane's face, but her expression was pleasant, almost peaceful. "If someone gave me a million dollars," she said, "I'd give it to my daddy so he could quit his drywall job and we could be a family all day long, all the time."

I crossed my arms in defeat. Lacey Jane might edge me out on the interview part. But I still had her beat on talent and appearance.

We heard voices outside.

"Oh, law." Miss Odenia sighed. "Here comes Viola Sandbanks and Palmer, and I'm not near ready. You know Viola is always the first to arrive anywhere so she can get the most comfortable chair. I really think I'm tired of playing cards."

It was after five when me and Lacey Jane finished drying the dishes.

"You girls run along now," Miss Odenia said. "Thanks for serving. Don't forget, tomorrow is dress rehearsal. Be here at ten."

"I'll bring those sandals over for you," Lacey Jane said as we stopped in the yard between our trailers. The sun was a red ball hovering over the sewer pipe. Even when it set, it wasn't any cooler.

"Okay. If you see Doublewide, grab him and call us!"

I had barely put one toenail across the threshold when Lynette yelled, "*Where* have you been?"

"I had a pageant lesson at Miz Odenia's. And then me

and Lacey Jane served at her card party. Didn't Rudy tell you?"

Rudy sat at the kitchen table, drawing and swinging his feet.

"He told me you went off with Lacey Jane—"

"Rudy!" I said. "Why didn't you tell your mother *every-thing* I told you?"

"I forget." He held up a comic of a cat wearing a cape. "Look what I made for Doublewide for when he comes home."

I turned back to Lynette. "You didn't take Rudy out to look for his cat?"

"No, I did not!" Her hair stood on end and her eyes were red-rimmed. "Do you remember me saying I had a great big huge exam I had to study for? You should have been keeping Rudy busy."

"Excuse me, but you didn't tell me to."

"It's your *job*, Rebel! I shouldn't have to tell you!"

I'd had enough of Lynette fobbing her work off on me. "What isn't my job around here? I make the beds and clean your grungy hair out of the sink and pick up Rudy's dirty clothes and fix lunch and supper plus watch him while you're gone all day—"

"That's what you're *supposed* to do!"

"You didn't tell me I'd have to be the maid. I was supposed to babysit Rudy—"

"*Which* you neglected to do."

"One lousy afternoon!"

Lynette slammed her fist on her stack of papers. "This is so like you, Rebel! You do whatever you want, whenever you want. You always have."

"Are you gonna drag out that Mama's-little-baby stuff again?" I said. "I can't help it I'm the youngest."

"You can help being the biggest brat in the United States! But I guess I can't blame you entirely. Mama and Daddy spoil you because you're the only one left at home."

"Well, there you go." I threw my hands out, palm up. "If Mama and Daddy spoil me, it's not my fault, is it?"

"I thought you'd grow up this summer. Accept some responsibility. Do you know what *I* was doing at your age? Mama had me cooking and helping her with the cleaning—"

I rubbed my forefinger and thumb together. "Eeeee," I sang shrilly. "This is the world's tiniest violin playing 'My Heart Bleeds for You.'"

Rudy stared at us. "Mama. Rebel. Please don't fight. It makes my spleen ache."

"We're not fighting, Rudykins. We're just—discussing something." Lynette rounded on me. "Be your bratty self. See where it gets you in life. Maybe one day Mama will be sorry she babied you so much."

I stopped playing my violin. "That's it! You're *jealous* of me! I bet you hated it when I was born, didn't you?"

Lynette flopped down in a chair. "You have no idea

what it was like. I was fourteen years old. I had—girl problems. All teenage girls do. And there was my mother—my *mother*—having a baby! It was so embarrassing."

"You told me you were thrilled when I was born!"

"I was, after I got over being embarrassed. Lord, you were a chunk. Did you know you weighed ten pounds, three ounces when you were born?"

"Is that a lot?" Rudy asked.

"Yes, it's a lot. Rebel was a lard bucket!" Lynette laughed.

"I was not!"

"You were so big, Daddy had to build a cart so Mama could haul you around the house. Nobody could carry you! You about broke our arms."

"A cart!" I said, insulted. "You're exaggerating."

"No I'm not. Mama's got pictures." Then Lynette frowned. "You know, Rebel, you grew up different from the way I grew up."

"Different how?"

"Mama and Daddy didn't have hardly any money when they first started out. Mama shopped at the thrift store for our clothes. We had fried Spam or grilled cheese three nights a week until Daddy got a promotion at Weber Tire and Auto. I remember wanting a chemistry set for Christmas. I asked for it every year, but I never got one."

This was news. "A chemistry set? I thought you liked girly stuff."

"You don't know everything about me, Rebel. Anyway, after I was married, Daddy got promoted to manager and the money situation eased up a lot." She sighed. "They were able to buy you things I didn't get, like store-bought clothes and more toys for Christmas. I think that's why Mama lets you get away with murder."

"I don't get away with murder," I said. "She made me come here this summer, didn't she?"

Lynette didn't hear me. "I don't want that to happen to Rudy. I don't want him to suffer because there isn't enough money. That's why I'm going to beauty school. I want to make a good life for us."

Rudy crawled into her lap and wrapped his gangly arms around her neck. "You're the best mama in the whole wide world."

"Only because I have the best boy in the whole wide world."

I blinked and looked away. I'd never realized Lynette's life was so different from mine. And that she was afraid she wasn't a good enough mother to Rudy.

"I'll watch Rudy more," I said. "And I'll clean up and do the dishes and stuff. If you promise me one thing."

"What?" Lynette asked.

"Don't tell anybody—I mean *nobody*—that I weighed ten pounds when I was born."

"Ten pounds, three ounces," she corrected. "Deal."

"Mama, are we going to drive around and look for

Doublewide, like you said?" Rudy asked.

Before Lynette could reply, the phone rang.

"Somebody found Doublewide!" Rudy shrieked in Lynette's ear.

"Gracious, Rudy, you deafened me," she said. "It could be Chuck. He's supposed to call right about now. Rebel, you're closest to the phone. You answer it."

I snatched up the receiver. "Hello?"

But it wasn't Chuck or anyone calling about finding Doublewide. I hung up the phone. "Just some guy selling insurance."

Rudy's face went slack and I knew he was about to cry. The poor kid couldn't catch a break.

"Listen, Rudy, let's walk around the neighborhood and ask people if they've seen your cat," I said.

"No, we'll drive," Lynette said, gently shoving him off her lap. "We'll cover more territory that way."

"What about your test?" I asked. "Don't you need to study?"

"My head is packed as full as it can get. If I cram in one more fact, it'll all come falling out." She picked up her purse and keys.

We drove up and down every single street in Grandview Estates and even by the houses on the other side of the trailer park. We stopped a lot of people, but no one had seen a large brown cat with a fake ruby collar.

Rudy sat in the front seat and cried all the way home.

Lynette rubbed his back until his sobs dwindled to hiccups. At home, she put him to bed.

"Here," I said, tucking Tusky under his arm. "I haven't been a very good friend to Tusky lately. He'll like you better."

Then Lynette and I folded laundry in the kitchen.

"Where do you suppose that cat is?" she said. "I hope he hasn't been hit by a car. That would smash Rudy's fragile little heart into a thousand pieces."

I didn't mention his father was already doing that by not calling when he said he would. But Lynette knew that.

"I don't know," I said. "Doublewide lives for food. You don't think he's so weak from hunger he can't stagger home?"

"That animal could live off the fat of the land for weeks. But I wish he'd come back. The place isn't the same without him."

I held up a pair of underpants. "Whose are these? They have a big hole in the seat."

Lynette snatched them away from me. "Mine. I can't afford to buy new ones."

"Oh. At least they're air-conditioned."

She giggled. "The only thing around here that is!"

"If you had a million dollars, what would you spend it on?" I asked.

She didn't even think. "I'd buy a house first. And a new bedroom suite. The water bed is getting old."

"Underpants?"

Suddenly we heard a loud, echoing *uuurrrrrrrrpppp!* from Rudy's room.

"What on earth—?" Lynette began. "Rebel, did you teach my child that disgusting habit?"

"Way to go, Rude!" I yelled. "At least a twenty-four-seconder!"

Bambi Lovering's
EXPERT BEAUTY TIPS

☀ *SUMMER EDITION* ☀

*D*oes your hair frizz like Brillo in the summer humidity? You don't have to go out in public with Bride of Frankenstein hair, like a certain person who's trying to be a beautician. (P.S. Always look at the hair of your hairdresser. If it's a rat's nest, don't walk, *run* to another beauty parlor!)

If you weren't blessed with natural curls like me, frizzy hair can cause needless heartbreak. But help is right here! Just try my foolproof tricks:

1. When you wash your hair, rinse it in cold water. Cold as you can stand.

2. While your hair is wet, use hair set tape all along the bottom (stick it to your neck or back if you have long hair). Your hair should dry straight.

3. For extreme cases, comb your wet hair in your normal style. Stick it down with hair tape. Then put a whole bunch of metal clips in your hair. Your head will look like a space alien helmet, so don't let anybody see you. But your frizz will be gone!

Frizz *can* be tamed and you never have to look scary!

Until next time . . . smile pretty!

*B*ambi Lovering,
Your Expert Beauty Consultant

FOURTEEN

Dobulewide Seeks His Fortune

Rudy sorted through a bowlful of dry Alpha-Bits. "Rebel, how do you spell 'Doublewide' again?"

"D-O-U-B-L-E-W-I-D-E."

"I can't find a *u*. Or another *d*." He looked like he was going to bawl again, so I dumped the cereal on the table.

"Flip this *p* around and it's a *d*." I sifted some more. "They probably didn't put any *u*'s in the box." I found an *h* and bit off the top part. Then I turned it upside down. "One *u* for you."

Lynette appeared in her smock. This morning her hair looked like she'd combed it with a tornado. "Rudy, you're supposed to be eating, not playing."

"If I get Doublewide's name, he'll come back today," he said, lining up his letters.

Lynette glanced at me over Rudy's head, planted a

lipsticky kiss on his cheek, then unlocked the front door. A piece of pink paper fluttered to the floor. "What's this?"

"Probably an ad for mowing lawns," I said, though I recognized Bambi's calling card.

"It's from that prissy girl across the street." She laughed. "What kids won't think of." Then she stooped and checked her reflection in the toaster. "What's wrong with my hair?"

"Nothing," I said. "Don't pay any attention to Bambi. She's not all there."

"'*Trying* to be a beautician'? I ought to speak to that girl's mother, who by the way, has the worst dye job ever. Every time I see her I feel like saying, 'Pick a color!'"

She wadded up the paper and left for school in a huff.

I was reading the latest issue of Bambi's Beauty Tips when Lacey Jane came in. She carried the plastic bag from the bridal consignment store and a shopping tote.

"Dress rehearsal day," she sang. "I brought your sandals and some white barrettes with turquoise flowers that match your dress perfectly. If you want to wear them." She read the piece of paper. "Lynette was the target this time."

"Yeah. She laughed, but I could tell she didn't think it was a bit funny." I glanced at Rudy, who had spelled *dobulewide* with the Alpha-Bits. "Rude, eat your cereal. We have to leave for Miss Odenia's."

"Rebel, can we go look for Doublewide again? Please?"

He had purplish smudges beneath his eyes from worrying over that cat.

"We don't really have time," Lacey Jane said to me. "Miz Odenia is expecting us at nine."

"Pleeeease, Rebel?"

"Rudy, your cat's been missing two days," Lacey Jane said brusquely. "When something is gone, it's gone."

Behind his glasses, Rudy's eyes grew watery. "Don't say that! Doublewide is my best friend!"

I made a slicing motion under my chin so Lacey Jane would shut up. "She didn't mean it the way it sounded, Rudy. *Right*, Lacey Jane?" I don't know what got into her sometimes. Granted, Rudy was an oddball, but he was still just a little kid.

"Um—Doublewide isn't really gone," she back-pedaled. "He's . . . seeking his fortune. You know, like a cat in a fairy tale."

Rudy scrubbed his eyes with his fists. "Really?"

"Yeah," I said, brushing the cereal letters back into the box. I left Rudy's *dobulewide* on the table. "Let's go look for him anyway. Okay?"

We trooped outside into the searing heat.

"Doublewide!" I felt a little ridiculous yelling the name of a trailer in a trailer park.

"Double-*wide*!" called Lacey Jane. "Here, cat!"

Rudy cupped his hands like a megaphone. "Doubbbblewiiide! C'mere, boy!"

"Doublew—" Lacey Jane and Rudy yelled together.

"Shush!" With my superior hearing, I detected a faint sound. Was that a cat meowing on the other side of the fence between our yard and Lacey Jane's?

"What?" Rudy asked. "What is it?"

Then we all heard the sound of claws desperately scrabbling up the smooth boards. Brown paws hooked over the top of the fence. Doublewide's small head rose into view. He appeared to be struggling.

"DOUBLEWIDE!" Rudy shrieked, racing toward his cat.

"Rudy, wait!" I dashed behind him, remembering *Old Yeller* and other stories that involved painful rabies shots in the stomach and a bad end to the animal.

Lacey Jane lurched along beside me. "That cat must have eaten well, wherever he was. He's so fat, he can barely get over the fence."

By the time we reached the fence, Doublewide teetered on top on his little marble feet. But his head was still at a weird angle, like something was pulling him backward.

"Lacey Jane," I ordered, "be ready to catch the cat!"

I tore through the gate and around the other side of the fence. Doublewide's hind feet were slipping, and I could see why. Somehow the cat had gotten a hanging basket of geraniums snagged on his fake ruby collar!

"I'll try not to hurt you," I said to him, reaching through leaves and flowers to find the end of the chain snared around his collar. He actually sat still, even though my fingers working under his already-tight collar must have been uncomfortable. At last the chain snapped free, and Doublewide practically sailed over the fence.

"Rudy's got him!" Lacey Jane called.

I hurried back through the gate with the flower basket. "*This* is what was caught on his collar."

Hugging the cat, Rudy stared at the geranium basket in horror. "Poor Doublewide. It's my fault! I put the collar on him so he'd be pretty like Kissy."

"Don't blame yourself," I said, unbuckling the cat's collar. "You know he's always into stuff. I wonder how long he hauled that basket around."

We all looked at Doublewide, as if expecting him to answer. He purred loudly in Rudy's arms, relieved to have the basket and collar off.

"He's probably starving," I said. "Let's feed him and then get to Miz Odenia's."

Doublewide bolted a can of kitty tuna down so fast, I thought it would come back up again. (He was famous for throwing up on Lynette's bedspread.) He put one paw in the dish to keep it from sliding and licked the bowl until it shone.

Rudy lay on the floor beside him, stroking his broad brown back. "I think he lost weight, Rebel. I can feel his backbone."

"He'll gain it back," I said. "Big moocher like he is.

Okay, Rudy, Doublewide is full as a tick. He'll take a nap while we're at Miz Odenia's."

"I can't leave him!" Rudy said in alarm. "He just got back home."

"You can't stay here by yourself. You're coming with us. Now, get up."

Rudy wouldn't budge. I reached down and lugged him up. He hung on to Doublewide, who was washing tuna juice from his whiskers. It was like lifting a draft horse.

So when Miss Odenia opened her door, she was greeted by two pageant girls, a seven-year-old tagalong, and a cat with serious tuna breath.

"Sorry," I told her. "Doublewide just came home, and Rudy won't part with him."

"That's okay," she said. "They'll pad our audience. Girls, go into my bedroom and change. We'll rehearse interview and your talent."

Lacey Jane and I stood awkwardly in the hall.

"I'll change in the bathroom," I said. With all the petticoats and bows and stuff on her dress, Lacey Jane needed more room.

I was just slipping my summer-spread feet into Lacey Jane's white sandals when I heard her rustle down the hall. Leaving my shorts and T-shirt in a heap on the floor, I hurried out to the living room.

At first I thought a curtain factory had exploded. Then I made out pale red pigtails and matchstick legs poking out from bushels of pink lace and ruffles and ribbons. Lacey Jane's dress looked even uglier than it had in Better-Off-Dead.

"Oooh," Rudy said from the sofa, where Doublewide was spilled over his lap. "Lacey Jane, that's the dress you should—"

If I hadn't been clear across the room, I would have clapped my hand over Rudy's blubbery lips.

"—be laid out in."

"What?" Lacey Jane spun around like a life-size cupcake.

Miss Odenia jumped in. "He means parade! It's the perfect dress to *parade* around in. I agree, Rudy. Now, you be quiet so Rebel and Lacey Jane can rehearse. Rebel, you start."

First I did my pageant walk up and down, but when I tried to do a pivot turn, the bottoms of my shoes slid on the rug. I nearly did the splits instead.

"Darn shoes! Are you sure I can't go barefooted?" I asked Miss Odenia.

"Those look like brand-new sandals."

"They are," Lacey Jane said. "They're a little too small for me, so I never wear them."

"Scuff them in the gravel to rough up the soles," said Miss Odenia. "You'll be fine."

I wasn't so sure. Did Lacey Jane let me borrow slippery new shoes to wreck my pageant walk on purpose?

Next I answered the same interview questions and

then I did my recitation. Rudy clapped Doublewide's front paws together.

"Be sure and smile, Rebel, even while you're talking," Miss Odenia told me.

"My face hurts," I complained. I glanced at Lacey Jane. "*Don't* say it."

"But it *is* killing me."

I swung a punch at her and missed.

"Girls! Lacey Jane, go ahead."

She managed to do her pageant walk with only a little lurching, and twirled her pivot turns perfectly. She grinned like a jack-o'-lantern through the interview. But she would not perform her talent for us.

That meant she was going to dance to that weird country music song. I saw Miss Odenia shake her head. I wondered if she was worried Lacey Jane would make a fool of herself in front of everybody.

Well, I wasn't worried. Lacey Jane's disaster dress would keep her out of the running in the appearance category. If Bambi dragged out that same old ukulele number and Lacey Jane lumbered around to "Sweet Dreams," I had the talent part made in the shade. I just needed to work on my interview.

Did I feel guilty? A teeny bit. I liked Lacey Jane, even though she could be prickly at times. But I liked paleontology more, and this was my *only* shot at getting to that Kids' Dig in Saltville.

Suddenly, we were distracted by the sound of heavy trucks rumbling down Grandview Lane. I thought it was the fire engines returning to the station, but Rudy bounced off the sofa and ran to the window.

"The carnival's here!" Rudy cried.

We joined him, pushing Miss Odenia's yellow drapes back so we could all see.

Huge flatbed trucks and tractor trailers slowly followed one another down the road like a train of elephants. Parts of carnival rides were chained to the flatbed trucks. On the sides of the trucks gaudy sparkle-burst letters spelled WIZARD AMUSEMENTS, MIDLOTHIAN, VIRGINIA.

"Midlothian," Miss Odenia remarked. "That's near Terrapin Thicket. They must have a big carnival warehouse there."

"I thought the carnival starts Friday," I said.

"I guess they need a day or so to set it up," Miss Odenia said. "Look, Rudy, those are the cars for the Ferris wheel. Ercel and I would ride the Ferris wheel at the county fair. He'd motion to the operator to stall our car at the top and then he'd rock it to make me scream."

In the middle of the rolling trucks, a familiar rattletrap car sputtered and choked. The Clunker.

"Mama's home!" Rudy cried. He slammed outside, Doublewide trotting behind.

This couldn't be good. Lynette's school lasted till one, then she went straight to Hair Magic. She must have failed the big test, and Miss Dot had kicked her out. And Hair Magic probably fired her for being a dummy.

In Miss Odenia's bathroom, I shucked my pageant dress, zipped into my shorts and T-shirt, and ran out the door. "Gotta go."

"Practice your pivot turns," Miss Odenia called after me.

The Clunker's door was open. Lynette stood in the driveway still wearing her smock. She grasped Rudy's wrists and spun him around till his feet flew off the ground. Rudy's giggles filled the hot afternoon air like feathers.

Poor Lynette. Getting kicked out and fired must have made her snap her twig.

I rushed up. "Hey, Lynette. Don't you want to go inside?" *Where the neighbors can't see you?* I almost added.

"I passed!" she exclaimed, ending Rudy's spin with a hug. "Rebel, I got an *A*!"

"Really? I mean, great! But aren't you supposed to be at work?"

"The shop is closed today. The hairdressers are at a color class."

"Mama, guess what?" Rudy said, pulling at her smock. "Doublewide came home. He had a flower basket around his neck!"

"Well, bless his flea-bitten heart. Are you okay, big boy?" Lynette bent down to pet the cat. I'd never seen my sister so happy. "Now we have two things to celebrate. Let's go to Kline's Tastee Freez!"

Rudy jumped up and down like his pants were on fire. "Oh, boy! I want a strawberry sundae."

A vanilla twist cone dipped in chocolate sure would hit the spot for me.

Lacey Jane hurried down the walk, carrying our plastic dress bags like a banner. "Rebel, you forgot your dress!"

"We're going to Kline's to celebrate the return of Doublewide and my first *A*," Lynette told her. "Come with us. My treat. Do you need to call your father at work?"

"No. As long as I'm with a responsible adult, I can go places."

Lynette peeled off her smock and flung it in the car. It landed on the package panel in the back. "Let me put on some shorts first."

Ten minutes later, we all piled in the car.

"Lacey Jane, sit with me," Rudy begged.

I could tell by the way Lacey Jane was scrunched all the way over by the other window she'd rather I was sitting in the back with her.

Soon we were cruising down the road, windows open, radio blaring, eager to knock the temperature down a degree or two with Kline's famous frozen custard.

FIFTEEN

The Bump Road

Kline's Tastee Freez was on the other side of Red Onion, on Dogtown Road.

"Is there a real Dogtown?" Rudy asked Lacey Jane. "Do dogs live there?"

"Do frogs live in Frog Level?" From the sharpness in her voice, I knew she didn't want Rudy pestering her the whole way.

I was more interested in the blue-and-white-striped box on the seat between me and Lynette. "What's this? A present?"

"Sort of. You have to give it back," Lynette said.

"It's not a present if I have to give it back." I thumbed one corner of the lid.

"No peeking."

A sign caught my attention. 1800 RAY OF HOPE LANE.

The address of Red Onion Prison, where my convict friend Skeeter was paying his debt to society. As we passed the turnoff in a cloud of dust, I stared down the road. Pretty red flowers bordered a long, serious wire fence with a coil of barbed wire rimming the top. I'm glad they made the place homey.

I wondered if Skeeter would track me down for that twenty-dollar bet after he was sprung. Another reason I needed to win the pageant prize money. You don't want to be owing an ex-con.

It was probably only ten minutes but seemed like forever until I spotted the Tastee Freez sign, shaped like a giant soft-serve cone. Lynette parked in the gravel lot and we bailed out.

Rudy clutched the ledge of the walk-up window, sputtering, "I want—I want—I want—Mama . . . I want a strawberry sundae, only without—" Sometimes the kid was so wound up, he didn't make sense.

"I know," Lynette said patiently, taking her wallet from her purse. "Without strawberries."

"If you don't like strawberries, how come you're getting a strawberry sundae?" I asked him.

"Because I like pink ice cream."

Like Rudy, I knew what I wanted right away, but we had to wait while Lynette and Lacey Jane compared and discussed each item on the menu like we were at the last dinner on the *Titanic*.

"I didn't have lunch today," Lynette said. "A chili dog and a chocolate milk shake sounds good to me. Make up your mind yet, Lacey Jane?"

"I'd like a pineapple sundae with wet nuts." She glanced at Lynette. "If that's okay. Wet nuts are extra."

"No problem." Lynette placed our orders. "We'll eat at the picnic table under the tree over there."

Lacey Jane pulled a wad of napkins from the dispenser, then covered the top of the picnic table. "I don't like eating where birds have pooped."

"Who does?" I said.

When our orders were ready, I wrapped a bunch of napkins around my cone. The trick about the dipped twist cone was that the second you bit into that thin chocolate shell, the frozen custard inside melted like it was sitting on a radiator. For the next ten minutes I was in a licking race to keep an ice cream river from dribbling over my fingers.

Lynette wolfed her chili dog down in three bites, then sucked on the milk shake straw till her cheeks hollowed. Lacey Jane, who looked like an X-ray, scraped the plastic spoon at the bottom of her sundae cup before the rest of us had hardly started. Of course Rudy inspected every spoonful of his sundae to make sure no speck of strawberry had sneaked through. We would be there till the Tastee Freez closed.

"Okay, I'm done," I said to Lynette. "Now, show me the sort-of present."

Lynette went back to the car to fetch the box. "Since you won't let me do your hair for the pageant, I borrowed this for you."

She lifted the lid, revealing a hairy dark brown thing. At first I thought she'd stuffed Doublewide in the box. Gently, Lynette took the wig off its plastic stand and held up this marvel for us to admire. A bushel of teased hair rose from nose-grazing bangs and fell in a tangle of wild curls.

"One hundred percent human hair. None of your slick synthetic Dynel." She stroked the wig. "The hair came from women in southern Italy. They have wonderful, thick hair."

"Can I put it on?" Rudy said, reaching for the bangs with a sticky hand.

Lynette swung it out of his reach. "Sugar-pop, this isn't a play wig. And it's not even mine. It belongs to the beauty school. Miss Dot told us it cost one hundred and fifty dollars. I don't *dare* let anything happen to it."

"Don't worry. I'm not wearing that moth-eaten bath mat for one second," I said firmly.

"Just try it on," Lynette wheedled.

"Yeah, Rebel, try it on," said Lacey Jane. "Let's see how you look."

I sat on the picnic table bench, stiff as a statue, while Lynette pulled my ponytail up, then slid the wig over my head. The net cap the hair was sewed to itched something fierce. Plus, it was too big.

"It's slipping off," I said.

"Wait. Let me fix the hook thingies in the back." Lynette shoved my head forward and fiddled with something at my neck. Suddenly my ears felt like they were being cut off.

"Too tight!"

Lynette pushed out her bottom lip in concentration as she finger-fluffed the hair around my shoulders. "Rebel, you have to pay a price for beauty."

Lacey Jane snickered, but Rudy said, "Rebel, that's the way you should wear your hair when you're—"

"Never mind!" I knew he wanted me to wear this wig with the dress he'd picked for when I'm laid out in my casket.

"There! You look very grown-up." Lynette dug in her purse for a mirror. "What do you think?"

I parted the long bangs and peered at my reflection. It looked like a woolly mammoth was crouched on my head. "You've *got* to be kidding. Get me out of this contraption!" I tugged at the bangs.

"Careful!" Lynette unhooked the cap and took the wig off of me with a sigh. "All right. If you won't let me fix your hair, at least let me do your makeup."

Even though I thought I looked fine the way I was, my face would be stacked against Bambi's glamour-puss. Maybe I should accept Lynette's help. "Okay."

Lacey Jane picked at the edge of the splintered picnic

table, staying out of our conversation, but clearly listening.

"Would you like me to do your makeup, too?" Lynette asked her.

Lacey Jane's sallow face lit up. "Can I wear green eye shadow?"

"We'll see. Rudy, you don't have to finish your sundae if you don't want to. I bet you're tired. It's been a long day." Lynette dumped our trash while Lacey Jane and I stripped the napkins off the table and tossed them in the wire can.

Lynette came back and studied the wig in its box. Then she put it on her own head. "I miss being a brunette. Maybe I'll dye my hair back."

The sun had dipped behind the hills but it wasn't a bit cooler. A chorus of locusts shrilled from the trees. *Ree-ree-ree-ree-REE.*

"Summer's half over," Lynette said as we climbed in The Clunker.

My stomach did a little flip. August was almost here! In two days—two!—the pageant prize money would be mine.

I squeezed my eyes shut as Lynette put the car in gear and backed out of the parking lot. I pictured the cool blue mountains around Saltville. No sleepwalking and sleep-singing nephews, no barrette-wearing bullies, no prissy little Kissy dogs, no lost cats or sisters studying about acne, no *Bambi* . . . just me and a bunch of long-dead animals.

"C'n we go down the Bump Road?" Rudy asked.

I half turned in my seat. "How do you know about the Bump Road?"

"Mama drived me down it. It made my stomach fly up."

Lynette grinned at him in the rearview mirror. "That's right, buddy."

"What's the Bump Road?" Lacey Jane asked.

"A back road between Red Onion to Grandview Estates," Lynette replied. "We call it the Bump Road because there's a hill—"

"And if you speed up, the car sails over the hill and makes your stomach feel like it's floating," I said. "But how come you know about it?"

"Rebel, Daddy drove me on the Bump Road long before you were even thought of. Who do you think named it?"

We sailed along the narrow road, churning up red dust. Queen Anne's lace and blue-flowered chicory brushed the sides of the car. I reached out the window and grabbed a handful of leaves.

With one arm out the window and the other over the top of the steering wheel, Lynette settled back, the wind blowing her Italian-hair curls every which way.

"One time," she said, "Daddy took us on this road. We had just come back from Wells' Market. I had a little bag of Planters salted peanuts and an RC Cola."

"Don't tell me," I broke in. "You choked on the peanuts."

"Worse. Just as Daddy speeded up the hill, I dropped all the peanuts in the RC. When we went over the hill, I took a slug. Whoosh!" She waved her hands wildly. "RC flew up my nose and went all over the place!"

We all giggled.

"What did Mama and Daddy do?" I asked.

"Nothing. I had to wash the car when we got back home."

Rudy leaned forward. "Mama had the funnest times!"

"It wasn't much fun cleaning up gummy RC all over the floor and windows and seat cushion." Lynette peered through the windshield. "Okay, everybody. There's the hill. Sit back, Rudy-pie."

"This is gonna be so fun!" Rudy said, clutching Lacey Jane's shoulder.

She pushed him away. "Get over on your side."

Lynette's foot mashed the gas pedal. The Clunker zoomed up the steep hill like it had wings.

"Over the top!" she sang. "Hold on to your hats, everybody!"

The Clunker soared over the hill. Just as I felt my stomach elevator up like it always did, something solid and dark launched from the backseat and landed in Lynette's lap.

She screamed and jammed on the brakes. We hit the bottom of the hill with a sickening scrape of the front bumper and us pinned against our seat belts. For a split instant no one said anything.

Then Rudy let out a wail. "Mama's been kilt!"

I stared at Lynette. She was most definitely alive, but her blond hair was flat as a johnnycake. The large brown object in her lap stared at her in surprise.

"Doublewide!" we both cried at once.

"That stupid cat!" Lynette said.

"Mama!" Rudy sobbed. "She's dead!"

I spun around and got on my knees so I could see in the backseat. Lacey Jane wrapped her arms around Rudy.

"No, she's not," she said soothingly. "Your mama's fine. See?"

"But her head fell off!"

Lynette hands flew to her pasted-down hair. "Oh, my God, the wig!" She shoved Doublewide at me, then jumped out of the car and opened the back door on Rudy's side.

"Oh, Rudy-puppy," she said, picking up the wig, which had tumbled over Rudy's feet. "The dumb ol' wig fell off. I'm okay! Oh, my poor baby." She smothered him with kisses. "And look, Doublewide stowed away. Didn't he give us all a scare!"

"He must have gotten in the car and gone to sleep under your smock," I said. "And when we went over the hill, he woke up."

"That cat is more trouble than you can shake a stick

211

at," Lynette said, getting back in the car. "Everybody ready to go home? I know I am."

"You want to sit up front?" I asked Rudy. "I'll change places."

"No," he whimpered. "I want to stay here with Lacey Jane."

I glanced back. Rudy nestled against Lacey Jane, who still had one arm curled protectively around him.

"Don't worry, Rudy," she murmured. "Nobody's gonna bother you."

I turned around and faced front. When I left in August, I wouldn't have to worry about Lacey Jane picking on Rudy anymore. And I wouldn't have to feel guilty about Rudy. He probably wouldn't miss me much. Maybe not at all.

Instead of feeling relieved, I sulked. Rudy sure took to Lacey Jane quick.

Doublewide purred and "mixed biscuits" on my legs the rest of the way home. I scratched his chin and watched the summer darkness rush past.

Personality Profile—Aries (March 21–April 21)

Born under a fire sign, you are a force to be reckoned with. You are confident and have the internal resources to deal with new ideas and situations. Forthcoming and direct, you are also competitive, opinionated, and territorial about possessions. You are curious but easily bored and often leave projects unfinished.

Famous Aries people: Thomas Jefferson, Leonardo da Vinci, Harry Houdini, Adolf Hitler (Aries/Taurus cusp)

Personality Profile—Pisces (February 19–March 20)

Born under a water sign, you are perceptive, imaginative, and sensitive to the feelings of others. You lead a rich fantasy life and form deep bonds with animals. Sometimes too agreeable, you can be an easy target for bullies. Although you like people, you are more of a loner.

Famous Pisces people: Albert Einstein, Dr. Seuss, Michelangelo, Elizabeth Barrett Browning

---

Personality Profile—Leo (July 23–August 22)

Ruled by the sun, you are ambitious, independent, loyal, and generous. Young Leos have confidence beyond their years. You enjoy being in the spotlight and shine like the sun with an audience. Although you are outgoing, you can also be arrogant, bossy, and will try to control everything around you. You also can't take criticism.

Famous Leo people: Jacqueline Kennedy Onassis, Lucille Ball, Amelia Earhart, Henry Ford

SIXTEEN

The Guessing Man

"Where y'all off to?" Bambi asked as we strolled past her front yard.

She was turning no-handed cartwheels, one after the other like an acrobat. I wondered if she'd added a flip to her talent routine. I'd almost pay good money to see her swing the ukulele behind her head in the middle of a cartwheel while she crooned, "Yessir, that's my baby."

"We're goin'—" Rudy began.

"Be still," Lacey Jane said, nudging him.

Unless Bambi stood facing backward all day, she'd figure out soon enough we were heading down the hill to the fire station. No reason not to tell her.

"We're gonna watch them set up the carnival," I said.

Bambi wrinkled her nose. "But it's dirty and dangerous there."

"Exactly. Why else would we go?"

"You'll get in trou-ble." She dragged the last word out like a threat.

I folded my arms across my chest. "We won't get in trouble if a certain person keeps her blubbery mouth shut. Come with us."

Lacey Jane jabbed me in the ribs. "Rebel!"

"Don't worry. Bambi never does anything her mother doesn't want her to."

That riled Bambi. She stomped over to the sidewalk. "I do so do stuff Mama doesn't want me to. Just to prove it, I'll come with y'all."

"Nice going, Rebel," Lacey Jane muttered as Bambi joined us. Lacy Jane moved up to walk with me, leaving Bambi to amble along with Rudy.

"Maybe she'll get a job in the sideshow." We cracked up.

"I heard that." Bambi pushed her bangs back as we trudged down the hill. "What's so great about going to a carnival that isn't even open yet?"

"For one thing, the food people might give free samples. I can't wait to get me some nachos and a tutti-frutti snow cone." I smacked my lips.

"How perfectly disgusting," Bambi said, sounding like she was forty-five.

Rudy gazed at her, his eyes wide with puppy love. "You and me are together, ain't we?"

"Don't say 'ain't,' and we happen to be on the same

sidewalk, that's all," Bambi said.

The lot beside the fire station looked like somebody had been playing with giant Tinkertoys. Half-built rides rose from the trampled grass. Burly guys attached cars to the Tornado and Octopus. Merry-go-round horses waited to be fastened to the platform. Men yelled as a crane hoisted metal cages on a long silver tube.

"That's the Zipper," I said. "I'm gonna ride it first tomorrow. See, that middle piece goes around like a Ferris wheel and the cage things flip over and over. If you stand up—which you're not supposed to do—you can make the cage flip even when it's not moving."

"We won't have time for rides tomorrow," Bambi pointed out. "Unless you're dropping out of the pageant?" She arched one eyebrow at me.

"In your dreams. The pageant doesn't last all day. *After* you lose, me and Lacey Jane are gonna hit the rides."

"In *your* dreams if you think I'll lose." Bambi looked down at Rudy. "You want me to win, don't you?"

Rudy didn't say a word. It was obvious his loyalty to me and Lacey Jane clashed with his love for Bambi.

Between the rides, colorful tents and stands advertised funnel cakes, pizza, kettle corn, and snow cones. My mouth watered. Junk-food heaven!

Then I spotted a red-and-yellow wagon with a sign that screamed, FRIED OREOS! FRIED TWINKIES! ASK ABOUT THE FRIED SURPRISE!

"Hey, kid!" The guy behind the counter saw me staring. "Wanna try my latest creation?"

I sidled up to the serving window. "I don't have any money." (This was becoming my summer anthem. I should have it set to music and sing it everywhere I went: *"I don't have any mo-ney!"*)

"Since I'm cranking up the fat anyway, it'll be on the house," he said. Snake tattoos seemed to crawl up his thick forearms.

"What's the Fried Surprise?" Lacey Jane asked.

Snake Arms leaned forward. "My own invention. Even better than the Oreos and Twinkies. Fried MoonPies!"

"Ewww," said Bambi.

I thought it sounded good, but if I played my cards right, I'd get more than one free sample.

"Well," I drawled, "I've never had a fried Oreo or a fried Twinkie. I should try them first. You know, for comparison."

"Gotcha."

We hung over the edge of the counter, feet dangling, as we watched him open a pack of Oreos and roll six dark cookies in a sticky batter. He unwrapped a package of Twinkies and dipped one of the cakes in the same batter. Then he dropped the coated cookies and Twinkie in a vat of bubbling oil the size of a hog trough.

"Gross!" Bambi remarked. "All that grease is bad for your skin. It's bad for everything!"

"Bambi, don't be such a wet blanket," I said.

After a few minutes, Snake Arms fished the cookies and Twinkie out of the vat. He drained them quicker than a blink on paper towels, then tossed them in a bowl of powdered sugar.

Dumping the fried goodies in a red-and-white-checked paper basket, he handed it through the window to me. "Bone appetite. Let 'em cool a tad."

The soft, pillowy Oreos called to me. I picked one up, scorching my fingers, and bit down with a yelp. Boiling hot chocolate oozed from the doughy center.

"He told you to let them cool," Bambi said.

I stuffed the rest of the Oreo in my mouth just to show her I was no sissy. Lacey Jane and Rudy each took a bite. I polished off the other five cookies, then tackled the fried Twinkie. It didn't taste as great as it sounded.

Snake Arms pushed another checked paper basket across the counter. "Try my Fried MoonPie. It'll put hair on your chest!"

Rudy giggled. "Girls don't have hairy chests!"

"How would you know?" I said, giving him the eyeball. Truthfully, I was stuffed to the gills and more than a little sick. But the Fried MoonPie might be the most delicioso thing I'd ever eaten in my life.

It wasn't. I'd had better deep-fried potholders.

"Well?" Snake Arms wanted to know.

"It's good," I fibbed, choking on the steaming

marshmallow filling. "They should sell like hotcakes."

"You have powdered sugar all over your face," Lacey Jane said, handing me a napkin.

We walked away, me a little unsteady from so much sugar and grease.

"The Ferris wheel!" Rudy said, clutching Bambi's hand. "Will you ride on it with me? I'll make it stop at the very top and kiss you."

Lacey Jane and I gawked at him. The chocolate from his one bite of fried Oreo must have shot straight to his brain.

Bambi shrugged off Rudy's grasp. "You're way too young to be thinking about girls, though I can understand why you're love-struck on me. It happens all the time. But I don't kiss *little boys*."

Rudy slumped like somebody stuck a pin in him.

"I don't see any big boys breaking the door down to kiss you," I told Bambi. "Nobody would go near you with a ten-foot pole." Pulling Rudy aside, I whispered, "Trust me, she's not worth it."

"I thought she liked me," he said in a painfully small voice.

"Bambi only likes herself," Lacey Jane said.

Miss Priss had wandered down the midway. She stood in front of a bright green weight machine and fixed her hair in its purple-framed mirror. A sign with purple flashing lights read, FOOL THE GUESSER! AGE! WEIGHT! BIRTH

219

MONTH! WIN PRIZES! ONLY $3! Cheap Frisbees, gaudy straw hats, and plush neon monkeys were piled in baskets.

A bald man with a brushy mustache and a potato nose boomed through his clip-on microphone, "C'mon over, folks. If I can't guess your age within *two years*, your birth month within *one month*, or your weight within *three pounds*, you *win* the prize of *your choice*!"

"Cool!" Lacey Jane said. "A fortune-teller!"

Rudy ran up to the man. "Hey, betcha you can't guess my name!"

I collared Rudy. "He can't guess your name. And he's not a fortune-teller. Those are women who wear turbans and gold coin earrings. And they have a crystal ball."

"The little lady is kee-rect. I can't predict the future or guess your name but I can tell you those three things about yourself because I'm a people studier." His big face broke into a crinkly smile. "I even went to college to study people! Now I'm an expert in age, weight, and birth months."

"All right," Bambi said like she was doing him a favor. "Guess my age."

"No, dummy." I elbowed her. "He can *see* we're kids." I sized the guy up. "You do it sort of like math, don't you?"

"You mean statistics? No, I'm just a real good people-studier. How about I guess your weight, then?" he asked me.

"I don't have any money." I *really* should make up music for that song.

"The carnival isn't officially open—and you aren't supposed to officially *be* here," he said, "but this'll be on the house."

The Guessing Man gazed at the ground, deep in thought. He *did* look like he was figuring out a tough math problem. Then he looked up and took a stubby pencil and a tiny notepad from his pocket. He wrote on the notepad, tore off the top sheet, then slapped it on the back of his hand.

"How much do you weigh?" he said to me. "If I'm three pounds over or under, you get to pick a prize."

"Ninety-eight pounds."

He handed me the slip of paper.

"One hundred and thirteen! Woo-hoo! You lose!" I was heading for a yellow monkey when Bambi said, "How do we *know* what you weigh, Rebel?"

"Because that's what I weighed at the doctor's! You want me to prove it? All right!" I stepped on the scale. The needle below the mirror swung past the one hundred mark and rested on one fifteen and a quarter.

"You're almost as much fat as Doublewide!" Rudy said.

"These scales are rigged!" I waddled off the weight machine.

Lacey Jane giggled. "Rebel, the fried MoonPie did you in!"

All that grease started roiling around in my stomach, which was sticking out like a bowling ball.

"Me next!" Lacey Jane said. "Tell me what month I was born in."

The Guessing Man went through the same drill, staring at the ground, then writing on the notepad. "What month were you born?" he asked her.

"March."

He showed Lacey Jane the paper. *March* was scrawled on it.

After that, we all wanted our birth months guessed. The Guessing Man said Bambi was born in August, which she was, and Rudy was born in February, which he was. Then it was my turn.

While the Guessing Man studied his shoes, I sent him wrong-month thoughts to mess with his mind. *July! September! November! December! January! May!*

He handed me the paper. It said *May*.

"I was born in April!" I crowed. My wrong-month thoughts worked!

"That's within a month," the Guessing Man said. "What day in April?"

"The eighteenth."

"Ah! You're an Aries on the cusp of Taurus." He reached behind him for a box on a stool and handed us each a colored card. Lacey Jane's and Rudy's were both red.

"These are about your zodiac sign," the Guessing Man explained. "If your birthday is around the time when the sign changes, it's called being on the cusp."

Bambi, who nobody had paid attention to for at least three seconds, tapped the Guessing Man's arm. "We're in the beauty pageant tomorrow. Will you come watch?"

"Yeah," Lacey Jane said. "Can you tell us who's gonna win?"

"He's *not* a fortune-teller," I said. "He deals in facts."

Bambi gave him a big wink. "We all know who deserves to win."

"It sure isn't you!" I wished I had a fried MoonPie to smush in her face.

The Guessing Man made a time-out signal. "I'll watch if I can get away. But I can see you are all winners."

"Even me?" Rudy asked.

Lacey Jane snorted. "You aren't even *in* the pageant."

Rudy wouldn't let it go. "But if I was, do you think I'm a winner?"

The Guessing Man cuffed him lightly on the shoulder. "Especially you, tiger."

We stopped in the fire station break room to get out of the sun and read our zodiac cards.

"I don't believe in this junk," I said. "Hey! Mine says I am confident and have internal resources to deal with new ideas and situations. Maybe there *is* something to this astrology stuff."

Lacey Jane leaned over. "It also says you are competitive, opinionated, and territorial about your possessions. In other words, you're stingy. And you have a cusp birthday with Hitler!"

"Hitler!" Bambi cackled. "*My* famous zodiac person is Jackie Kennedy Onassis."

Rudy breathed down my sweaty neck. "Read mine, Rebel."

"Ours are the same," Lacey Jane said. "We're perceptive, imaginative, and sensitive to the feelings of others. We lead a rich fantasy life and we form deep bonds with animals."

"What does that mean?" he asked.

"We like animals and they like us." She frowned. "I am *not* an easy target for bullies."

Rudy nodded. "Doublewide and me get along real good."

I never realized how much Rudy and Lacey Jane had in common. Rudy was an easy target for *her* bullying. And Little Miss Goldilocks picked on Lacey Jane.

Bambi read from her card. "'You are ambitious, independent, loyal, and generous.' So true."

"Oh, please," I said. "You're only loyal to Bambi Lovering."

She went on. "'Young Leos have confidence beyond their years. You enjoy being in the spotlight and shine like the sun with an audience.' Right again."

I grabbed her card. "It also says you're arrogant, bossy, and a control freak."

We fell silent then, sitting in the cool dimness of the break room. Outside, carnival workers barked orders and hammers rang on metal. The firemen waxed the ladder truck.

I riffled the edges of my astrology card. I used to think I was the most special person in Grandview Estates, but now I wasn't so sure. It seemed like everybody here was special in their own way, even Rudy.

Bambi was a royal pain, but she had talent and was going after her life goals, dumb as they were. Lacey Jane believed in dreams and Miss Odenia's Marriage Turtle. Rudy loved people who didn't love him back, like Bambi and his own father. It took nerve to do that.

Tomorrow was the beauty pageant. Only one of us would win in our category.

The most special, talented person of all.

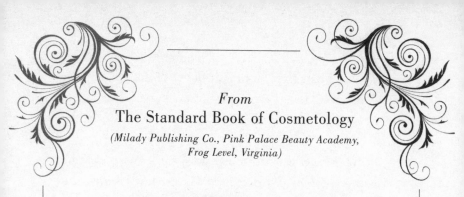

From
The Standard Book of Cosmetology
*(Milady Publishing Co., Pink Palace Beauty Academy,
Frog Level, Virginia)*

❧ *Eye Makeup* ❧

Eye makeup is applied for the purpose of improving the appearance by emphasizing the good points and making defects less conspicuous.

Eye shadow, when applied to the upper lids, complements the eyes by making them look brighter and more expressive. The daytime shade of eye shadow should be more subtle, whereas the nighttime shade can be a bit more daring.

Small eyes. Small eyes can be made to appear larger by extending the shadow slightly above, beyond, and below the eyes.

Close-set eyes. For eyes that are set too close together, apply shadow lightly up from the outer edge of the eyes.

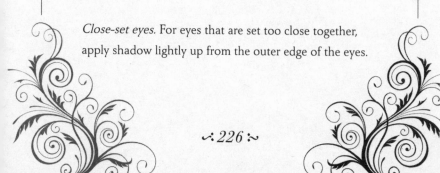

Eyes set too far apart. For wide-set eyes, use the shadow on the upper inner side of the eyelid.

Mascara is applied to the eyelashes to make them look fuller and longer. Use black mascara only on black lashes; otherwise, use brown mascara.

Swish the mascara wand horizontally across the lashes, wiggling the brush in an upward motion to prevent clumping.

SEVENTEEN

Bambi the Second

"Don't *move*," Lynette told me for the fiftieth time. She wiped my forehead roughly with a paper towel.

"I can't help it," I said. "You're jabbing that thing right in my eye!"

"I'm *not* jabbing it in your eye!"

"Well, it feels like it. You wear that goop all the time. I'm not used to it."

Blowing out a puff of air, my sister waved the mascara wand in front of my face. "Did you hear Lacey Jane whine when I put mascara on her? Did she blink and jerk away?"

"No, indeed," Lacey Jane said, already made up and calm as a button as she leafed through Lynette's cosmetology textbook.

Rudy rummaged in Lynette's plastic tackle box of jars and bottles. "I think Rebel would look good in this stuff. Put some of this on her, Mama."

"Honeybun, Rebel can't wear Black Pearl eye shadow. It's way too old for her."

I wrinkled my nose at the tiny pot Rudy had opened. "Looks like coal dust. Over my dead body will you stick that on me."

"I ought to, if you keep carrying on." She clicked open a tiny case and swept a soft little brush over my eyelids. "This is Max Factor's Peaches 'N Cream. Perfect for brown eyes. Plus you won't look like a tramp."

"It says here," Lacey Jane said, "to make close-set eyes look bigger, you smear eye shadow from the outer edge of the eyes."

"Are you insinuating I have beady eyes?" I said.

"No, just reading." Lacey Jane gazed at her reflection in Lynette's round makeup mirror. "I think I'll wear eye shadow all the time. What's this color called again?"

"Satin Nightie," Lynette replied, swiping her pinkie finger at the corner of my eyes. "Pink brings out the green in your eyes. Green shadow would look too harsh."

"You're so smart about all this," Lacey Jane said wistfully. "How will I ever learn this stuff?"

"You have plenty of time." Lynette touched her shoulder. "C'mon over anytime you want and we'll talk makeup and hair."

We'd all been up since the break of day. The pageant started at eleven thirty, but Lynette had to work at Hair Magic till noon.

When Lacey Jane had arrived at six thirty, a dark cloud had followed her into our kitchen. She flung herself dramatically in a chair and said, "Daddy can't come watch me in the pageant. Some guy called off at work, and Daddy has to go in."

"Aw, sugar," Lynette had said. "I'll cheer enough for him and me, okay? Now, let's get started."

She had fixed my hair first, curling it under in a "classic bob." Not big at all. I actually liked it.

But when she picked up a wisp of Lacey Jane's limp red hair, Lynette frowned. "How'd you feel about me cutting it short?" she'd asked.

Tears welled in Lacey Jane's eyes. "My mother wanted me to have long hair."

"Then let me trim those split ends."

About a hundred years later, Lynette handed Lacey Jane the round mirror. Her hair fell from a side part with half tucked behind one ear. The other half curved around Lacey Jane's thin face. The haircut made her look older and not so homely.

Now Lynette said, "All right, Rebel, last chance." She made another pass with the mascara brush. I widened my eyes but at the last second pulled away. "Rebel! You're gonna make me late for work!"

"I'll do it myself," I said, taking the mascara tube from her.

"Don't put it on too thick," she warned, gathering up

her purse and keys. "And none on your bottom lashes. You don't want to look overdone. Miz Matthews is coming by at ten to help y'all get dressed."

"What am I supposed to do with Rudy while me and Lacey Jane are in the pageant?" I asked.

"I'll come straight from work," Lynette said. "If I'm a few minutes late, Miz Matthews will watch him. Don't mess up your hair, either of y'all!" Then she was out the door.

"I'm hungry," Rudy said, stacking the eye shadows and blushes from Lynette's makeup box into a tower.

I'd fixed us toast when we first got up, but that was ages ago. I set milk and Golden Crisp on the table, along with three bowls and spoons.

"I can't eat a bite," Lacey Jane said. "My stomach's too nervous."

"My stomach never skips a meal." I ate a big bowl of cereal and drank two glasses of milk, one after the other.

"Milk is gassy," Lacey Jane stated. "You'll probably make all kinds of weird noises onstage."

Rudy made farting sounds with his hand in his armpit, cracking himself up.

"Ha-ha," I said. "Can you rinse our bowls? Thank you." I uncapped the mascara brush and leaned into the mirror propped against the milk carton.

"According to the book, you're supposed to swish the brush sideways across your lashes, wiggling it through so you don't get clumps," Lacey Jane said.

"My eyelashes don't grow sideways. They grow straight out. That's how I'm putting this stuff on." I gripped the brush tightly and dragged it from the base of my eyelashes to the ends.

"Rebel, the mascara's all globby!"

"It'll dry okay." I stared at myself in the mirror. "My eyelashes are straight as pokers. I wonder how Lynette gets hers so curly?"

Rudy plucked a medieval-looking contraption from the box. "Mama uses this."

"What *is* that?" The bottom of the tool had loops to put your fingers in, like scissors. I opened and closed the mouthlike top.

"An eyelash curler. I've seen those," said Lacey Jane. "You slide the open part over your eyelashes and squeeze the handle."

"And it'll make my eyelashes curly?"

She nodded. "Longer and thicker, too. Go ahead, try it."

It wouldn't do to have skimpy eyelashes. Rabbit lashes, Bambi called them. She'd mentioned an eyelash curler in her beauty tips.

It looked safe enough. Holding the curler in the open position, I eased it over the eyelashes of my left eye.

"Like this?" I asked Lacey Jane, blinking like crazy.

"Yeah, but back farther. Where your eyelashes grow from your eyelid. And quit blinking."

Pretend you are digging up a *Toxodon*, I told myself. One of its fangs is broken in a million pieces. Move your hand very delicately—

Holding my breath, I squeezed the handle.

"Press again just to make sure," Lacey Jane urged.

This time I clamped down hard. Then I slowly opened the curler and moved it away from my eye, releasing my breath.

I stared at the tool in my hand.

The rubber pads of the eyelash curler wore a fringe of short hair, like a teeny tiny wiglet. I grabbed the mirror. My left eye had only about four stubby lashes.

"*Lacey Jane!*" I shrieked, jumping up. "My eyeball is *bald*! You said I'd have thick, curly eyelashes! I don't have hardly *any*!"

Lacey Jane examined the hairy eyelash curler. "Hmm. Maybe you weren't supposed to use this after you put on all that mascara—"

"*Now you tell me!* What am I gonna *do*? We have to be at the pageant in"—my glance flicked to the clock over the sink—"less than two hours!"

"There's only one thing you can do," she said soberly. "Pull out all your lashes so your eyes match."

"*What?*" I turned around. "Rudy, is there a sign on my butt that says 'Kick Me'?"

"I don't see one—"

I whirled on Lacey Jane. "You did this on *purpose*. 'Go

233

ahead, try it.' You let me jerk all my eyelashes out because you want to make sure I'll lose."

Lacey Jane stood up. "If that's what you think, Rebel McKenzie, then I'll drop out of the pageant that you begged me to enter."

Would she? I doubted it. Hanging around Lacey Jane was like walking on the edge of the La Brea Tar Pits. One minute you're on solid ground, the next minute you're sinking out of sight. It didn't pay to be friends with her, not even fake friends.

Using Lynette's tweezers, I pulled out each little hair from the eyelash curler and tried to stick them back on my eyelid. The lashes fluttered to the surface of the mirror like a bunch of parentheses.

"One eye seems bigger than the other," I muttered. "I'm Alien Girl."

"I told you what you should do."

If there was anything I hated more than Lacey Jane messing up my chances at the pageant, it was Lacey Jane being right.

With a sigh, I picked up the curler, slipped it over the lashes of my right eye, and squeezed hard. When I took the curler away, most of my eyelashes came with it.

Both eyes looked like buzzard's eggs.

When our doorbell rang, Rudy rushed to answer it. Miss Odenia came inside and right away noticed me sitting at one end of the sofa with Lacey Jane clear at the other end. I wore a tea towel draped over my face, but I could feel her stare.

"You two fell out," she proclaimed.

"*Some*thing fell out," I said sourly.

"Over the pageant, I bet," she went on. "Rebel, you don't have to worry about a draft indoors."

I snatched the towel off my head and glared at her. "No, but I *should* have worried about back-stabbers."

Miss Odenia stopped short when she saw my nearly naked eyeballs. "Oh, my."

"I did *not* stab you in the back," Lacey Jane said. "You should have followed the instructions."

"There weren't any. Anyway, *you* seemed to know all about how to use an eyelash curler. What are you, Bambi the Second? Since when do you know so much about makeup?"

"Girls!" Miss Odenia held up one hand like a policeman. "Rebel, these things happen—"

"But not right before a beauty pageant!"

"Oh, yes they do. Even makeup artists make mistakes. I've seen girls go to a photo shoot looking like zombies. Mistakes can be fixed."

"Not this one," I said glumly.

Miss Odenia came over and tipped my chin up. "Okay, you'll have to live with this particular mistake. But you don't have to let it get you down. Appearance is only one third of the pageant score. And beauty isn't just eye shadow and lip gloss and hair spray. It's who you are. Let the judges see the real Rebel McKenzie."

"I don't suppose I can hold a picture of me when I had eyelashes over my face?" I asked hopefully.

"Nope. Go get your dresses. Time to get ready."

Lacey Jane cut in front of me as we hurried down the hall to Lynette's bedroom, where our dresses were hanging. I clipped her out of the way to reach the closet first. Our eyes locked, but we didn't say one word to each other.

War had already been declared.

EIGHTEEN

Dryer Sheet Curls and Vaseline Teeth

The air over the carnival grounds shimmered with excitement.

Toy pistols at the shooting gallery cracked and popped. Teenage boys in muscle shirts swung the mallet overhead, trying to hit the strongman gong. The merry-go-round played a tinselly tune as little kids ran to pick their horses.

Miss Odenia smiled wistfully up at the Ferris wheel. The ride wasn't moving, but the top car—the one her friend Ercel would rock to make her scream—seemed to touch the low, white sun.

"The stage is set up over there." Miss Odenia steered me, Rudy, and Lacey Jane across grounds littered with straw.

My palms were slick, but I couldn't wipe them on the skirt of my pageant dress. "Miz Odenia, do you have a Kleenex?"

She glanced at me. "Uh-oh. We need to fix your melting makeup. Your face looks like a Hostess cupcake in Death Valley."

Comments like that filled me with *all* kinds of confidence.

"How about my face?" Lacey Jane asked frantically. "Is my makeup okay?"

"You must tolerate the heat better than Rebel," Miss Odenia said, blotting my forehead with a tissue, then giving me another to pat my hands.

The folding chairs in front of the stage were filled with picture-snapping parents. Also people we knew. Viola Sandbanks sat front-row center, flapping a funeral home fan. Her mouth twisted in annoyance, either at the sweltering heat or the sight of her daughter Palmer cozied up to Mr. Beechley two seats away. He looked a little green, but maybe he was the type that didn't do well in the heat either.

Rudy spotted the woman who won big at bingo every week and the man with the football-shaped thing on his neck. Rudy ogled the man until Miss Odenia said it wasn't polite to stare and that poor Mr. Lake couldn't help it he had a goiter.

In the very front, two men and a woman sat at a table with notepads, pencils, and grim expressions. I'd seen happier grave diggers.

"The judges," Miss Odenia told us.

We found Mrs. Randolph, the world's oldest and smallest pageant director, scurrying back and forth onstage. A whistle swung from a lanyard around her neck.

"Sweet Peas over here!" she yelled, raising her arm to reveal a pit stain the size of North Carolina.

Little girls in poufy skirts and clackity patent leather shoes milled around like baby chicks. Their mothers fluffed curls and yanked dress-tails down over ruffled underpants.

Fweeeet! Mrs. Randolph blew her whistle so hard, her face turned as red as a pickled beet. "Line up, Sweet Peas!" Her whistle shrilled again, and a couple of the little kids' faces puckered up.

A teenage girl with craterlike acne (obviously not a contestant) told us in a bored monotone, "All contestants wait under the tent till their group is called. There's cold drinks in the cooler. And a Johnny-on-the-Spot over by the Tub O'Fun if you have to go."

The tent was behind the stage. Girls sat at picnic tables while their mothers fussed over them.

"I'll see to you girls," Miss Odenia said. "Then Rudy and I'll go out front." She checked the program the girl handed her. "Sweet Peas are first. They don't have a talent category. The Daisies go next—appearance and talent. According to this schedule, you Violets are on at twelve thirty. Lacey Jane, I'll give that girl your music."

She kissed us both on the cheek and left with Rudy. I slipped around to the side so I could see.

Music blared from speakers on either side of the stage. Dressed in a white suit with a baby-blue shirt and baby-blue *shoes*, Mr. Randolph, owner of the pest control part of Better-Off-Dead, hopped up onstage like a flea on a hot greased griddle. His loose stomach jiggled as he danced around with his microphone, grinning at the crowd.

"All righty, folks, let's get the third annual Miss Frog Level Volunteer Fire Department beauty pageant *rollin'*!" He spoke so loud, spit sizzled on the microphone, which he didn't even need.

"This year's pageant, like last year's and the year before's, is brought to you by those fine people at Better-Off-Dead Pest Control and Bridal Consignment, owned and operated by yours truly and my mama, Mrs. Maybelline Randolph! Give Mama a big hand, folks! She's worked like a mule plowing potato hills to make this pageant happen."

Everyone clapped and cheered.

"We'll begin with the sweetest young'uns this side of heaven," Mr. Randolph yelled. "Anita! Music, please!"

The crater-faced girl pushed some buttons on the sound system and a song about the good ship *Lollipop* drooled from the speakers. The Sweet Peas straggled across the stage, not looking at the judges or where they were going. They started and bumped into each other like train cars switching tracks. Finally Mrs. Randolph got them herded at one end. The first Sweet Pea scuffed to the center of the stage.

"What's your name, sweetheart?" Mr. Randolph boomed.

The girl stuck her finger in her mouth.

"C'mon, honeypie, tell these fine folks your *name*. I bet it's as pretty as you are."

The girl's mouth formed a square as she began to howl, mascara streaking down her heat-flushed cheeks. Her mother rushed onstage and hauled her off.

Mr. Randolph faced the audience and said, "She told me her life's ambition is to spread joy to everybody she meets. Give that little lady a big hand!"

I'd seen enough. I went back around to the tent.

Even though we weren't speaking, Lacey Jane turned to me and said, "This pageant has no place to go but up." She was right about that.

The other Violets joined us. Four of them were so much alike—blond ponytails, blank blue eyes, and bland personalities—that I called them all by the same name. Chanel-Winter-Baylee-Shelbylynn. Definitely no threat.

Then Bambi Lovering's mother strode into the tent as if clearing trash from her precious daughter's path. The two glasses of milk I drank earlier churned in my stomach. Lacey Jane's eyes widened and the Chanel-Winter-Baylee-Shelbylynns gasped.

Bambi was a puredee sight to behold.

Her hair was impossibly golden, perfectly curled, and very big. A village of chipmunks could have lived in that hair. Her cheeks blushed a rosy color. Creamy shadow made her eyelids glow like pearls. Lynette would say Bambi was "overdone," but the judges would think she was pretty from where they sat.

And her dress! Made of soft pink material that seemed to float, the long skirt stood out like a ball gown. Sparkly pink beads formed flower designs all over the top, which circled her neck in a halter style. Long see-through gloves like pink cobwebs covered her arms. Clear sandals with a strip of pink rhinestones peeked out from beneath the hem. Bambi's toenails and fingernails matched her dress.

Next to Bambi's dazzling outfit, Lacey Jane's dress was a pink nightmare.

Bambi's mother set a tote bag on one of the tables. A little furry head popped up and Kissy scrambled out. Her toenails matched Bambi's dress, too.

Bambi flashed me her famous pageant smile. "You *did* show up."

"Why wouldn't I?" I said. She wasn't going to scare me off even if her Cinderella gown made me feel a little dowdy.

"For one thing, your face looks like it got caught in a blender—"

"Bambi," her mother said sharply. "No talking to the other contestants. You need to save your voice. Now, hold still."

She took out a box of dryer sheets from the tote bag.

The rest of us Violets gaped as Mrs. Lovering wiped each of Bambi's curls with a dryer sheet.

"So my curls won't frizz in this humidity," Bambi explained. "It's one of the tips in my book—"

"Shh," her mother said, whisking a tube of lip gloss from the tote. She applied pink gloss to Bambi's lips, then stood back and frowned, like she was grading a science project. "Good. Remember, don't sit down, don't drink anything, and don't speak to the other girls. Bare your teeth."

Bambi pulled her lips back like a snarling wildcat. Uncapping a jar of Vaseline, her mother swiped a fingerful of the icky stuff over her front teeth. Then she scooped up Kissy, who was busy smelling everyone's feet, and plunked her back in the tote.

After her mother left, Bambi said, her lips sliding like ball bearings on ice, "Schkeeps your schmile from schticking."

"Are you going to talk like that in your interview?" I asked.

"Schome of the schlickness will schwear off by then."

We peeked out at the stage. The Sweet Peas were toddling down the steps. One dragged a huge ribbon sash like a too-big diaper. The Daisies filed onstage to their music.

While the Daisies answered questions from the judges, the Chanel-Winter-Baylee-Shelbylynns chattered about school and swim team practice and movies. The Rose girls—the teenage category after us—came in, tanned and gorgeous. They sat together and ignored us Violets.

Lacey Jane picked at her fingernails. I went over my recitation, neatly written out on notebook paper. To make sure I wouldn't stumble over the prehistoric names, those words were printed in red ink. Bambi tuned her ukulele.

Mr. Randolph announced the name of the winning Daisy. From where I sat I couldn't see the winner being crowned, only the disappointed backs of the losers.

Suddenly the whistle shrilled and Mrs. Randolph screeched, "Violets onstage! Line up in alphabetical order! Walk out and turn, then walk back."

Lacey Jane shot me a look. I thought she might say, "Good luck," but she silently took her place at the end of the line, behind one of the Chanel-Winter-Baylee-Shelbylynns. Bambi Lovering flounced in front of me. The other three C-W-B-S girls went ahead of her.

We pageant-walked straight across the stage. I remembered to keep my head toward the judges and smiled so wide the edges of my mouth cracked. The judges sat like crows on a fence.

I was doing great until the pivot turn at the far end of the stage. Bambi's long dress swished behind her like a fishtail, and I stepped on the hem. Her head jerked back, but she kept her balance, her smile never slipping as she hissed, "Nice going, klutz!"

Rattled, I reversed the pattern of the pageant-walk, balancing on my heel instead of the ball of my foot. I clumped back across the stage as if I were wearing army boots. Through her ever-present smile, Bambi went, "Hee-hee."

I mustered up the nerve to check out the audience. Lynette sat in the second row, between Miss Odenia and Rudy. She gave me a thumbs-up.

"Now it's time to meet this bee-oo-ti-ful bunch of girls," Mr. Randolph boomed. "Come on up, sweetheart, and tell the world your name and your life's ambition."

Baylee, the first of the Chanel-Winter-Baylee-Shelbylynns, marched up, stated her name, and announced she wanted to save Canada geese from being endangered.

"Well, that's real nice, Miss Baylee," Mr. Randolph said, "but I don't think Canada geese were ever in danger. I got so many in my back field, they look at me like *I* should be worried!" The audience laughed.

The next two C-W-B-Ss didn't do any better. They both giggled, and one of them couldn't remember her own name.

Then it was Bambi's turn. She glided to the front of the stage and dipped in a little curtsy.

"My name is Bambi Amberleigh Lovering," she said. "Amberleigh is spelled with an *l-e-i-g-h*, not your more common *l-e-e*." That settled, she added, "My life's ambition is to stop world hunger."

The audience murmured approval, and Bambi's smile brightened another fifty watts.

But Mr. Randolph didn't let her off the hook so easy. "An *admirable* goal, Miss Bambi Amber-l-e-i-g-h. Do you have a plan?"

"Oh, yes!" she said. "It's so *simple*—all we have to do is make an extra sandwich. Say you're fixing a peanut butter and jelly sandwich for school. Make *two* and send the other one to the hungry people!"

That was so beyond stupid I was amazed anyone clapped, but they did.

The woman judge jotted something on her notepad, ripped it off, and passed it to Anita, who gave it to Mr. Randolph.

He read the note, then said, "It seems we have one more question for you, Miss Bambi Amberleigh. Where did you get that very pretty dress?"

Wouldn't you know those hardhearted judges would think Bambi's dress was the fanciest?

"This old rag? It's been hanging in my closet for years." She smiled so bright, I was surprised the judges didn't get sunburned.

It was my turn. I walked up to the front of the stage. Lynette and Rudy waved like mad.

"What's your name, hon?" Mr. Randolph thrust the microphone under my nose.

"Rebel McKenzie," I said clearly. "No middle name spelled any which way." Lynette and Miss Odenia tittered, and Bambi's mother turned around to glare at them.

"Miss Rebel, tell everyone your life's ambition."

I had planned to say I wanted to work for world peace, but two of the C-W-B-S girls already took that one and it didn't go over so hot. I thought back to our interview practice. "Be specific," Miss Odenia had instructed. "And sincere."

"I want . . . to buy my sister some new underpants," I blurted. "Hers are all holey and stretched out. *And also*"— I spoke louder to be heard above the laughter—"*also* I want to make little tiny eyelash wigs for people who don't have any. Eyelashes, I mean."

"Very selfless," Mr. Randolph said. "And very . . . original. Give Miss Rebel a round, folks!"

Somehow I got back in line. I didn't hear what the last C-W-B-S girl said. All I could hear was my own voice talking about *underpants* and *eyelash wigs*!

"The crown is *mine*," Bambi whispered in triumph. "Not that you were ever any competition, bald eyes."

"It's not over," I whispered back.

Lacey Jane lurched to stand beside Mr. Randolph.

Mr. Randolph grinned down at her. "And last, but certainly not least, we have this charming young lady. Tell us your name and what you want to do in life."

"My name is Lacey Jane Whistle," she said. "In my life I want to—" She hooked her hair behind one ear nervously. "Wait a sec."

I could see Miss Odenia wince. She probably thought

Lacey Jane had forgotten everything she had ever taught her about interview questions.

"Take your time," Mr. Randolph said.

"I had this all figured out but it's kind of hard to describe." Lacey Jane took a deep breath. "Okay. I want to start a school—no, more like a club, only a nice friendly one—for girls who don't have mothers and need to learn how to do stuff like fix their hair. Older girls—ladies— will teach them about makeup and tell them when they're too old for ankle socks. And . . . that's what I want to do."

No one spoke. Then the applause exploded. Instead of smiling at the judges, Lacey Jane bit her lip and stared down at her sandals.

"All right, folks!" Mr. Randolph said, when the clapping faded. "We're gonna start the talent part of this pageant—"

A scream ripped through the audience. My sister stood up, clutching the strap of her purse in a stranglehold.

"Rudy's gone!" she cried. Everyone turned to stare at her. "My little boy is gone!"

NINETEEN

An Unexpected Contestant

"Rebel!" Lynette shrieked. "Get down here and help me find my baby!"

Mr. Randolph, who probably realized the lady in the audience was close to hysterics, said, "Folks, there seems to be a little trouble down front. What say we take a ten-minute break and help look for this missing infant?"

I scrambled off the stage and met Lynette's eyes. They whirled like twin pinball machines.

"He was sitting with me and Miz Odenia," she said, seizing my arm.

"Then how did he get away?" I asked.

"He got up to put his trash in the can. But he never came back! Rudy! Ruuudeee!"

I scanned the crowd. I could hear people asking Miss Odenia for a description of the missing "infant." Between the rides and food stands and games, Rudy could be anywhere.

"Where *is* he?" Lynette screeched. "He's been kidnapped!"

"Maybe he went to the Johnny-on-the-Spot," I said. "You go check. It's by the Tub O'Fun. I'll look around the game booths."

But Lynette pulled me back. "That'll take too long! Come with me to the missing child station. And then we're calling the police."

A man hurried up, towing a blond-haired little boy. "Is this your son, miss? I found him wandering around the pony ride."

"That's not Rudy! My baby boy is sweet and kind and much *better looking* than that boy ever will be!"

The little boy's face screwed up like he was going to cry.

"Lynette, get a grip!" I said as the man led the boy away. "Or the police will take *you* to jail."

I caught a glimpse of something near the stage steps, a small, pale figure with white-blond hair and taped glasses. He wore a plastic inner tube around his waist and gripped a shiny black tote bag with something heavy inside.

"There he is!" I said. "There's Rudy!"

"Where—?" Lynette looked frantically in the direction I was pointing.

"We found him!" I yelled toward the stage.

Feedback from the microphone shrilled in our ears. Mr. Randolph adjusted the sound with an apologetic smile and announced, "Folks, the missing baby has been found. I repeat, the missing baby has been found. Return to your seats and we'll get this show on the road again!"

Lynette knocked people over as she rushed toward the stage, but Rudy had already climbed the steps. All of the Violets were in line except me. Rudy wedged himself between Lacey Jane and one of the C-W-B-S girls. I hurriedly took my place.

"Get that kid out of here," Bambi said, twitching her long skirt back like Rudy had flying cooties.

I leaned over. "Rudy! What in tarnation are you *doing*?"

"Rudy Eugene Parsley!" Lynette's voice carried over the music of the nearby merry-go-round. "Get off that stage right this minute!"

"No." Rudy shifted his grasp on the heavy bag, resting it on the inner tube around his waist.

Mr. Randolph ambled over. "Hi-dy, son. What's your name?"

"Rudy Parsley."

"Well, Rudy Parsley, we're having a beauty pageant. For young *ladies*."

The C-W-B-Ss giggled.

Rudy looked scared but stood his ground. "I have a talent. I don't see why I can't do it just because I'm a boy."

Mr. Randolph's sweaty face split into a grin. "That's a mighty good point." He turned to the audience. "What do you think, folks? Should we let this boy perform?"

The judges nodded and even cracked a tiny smile. Everyone clapped except Bambi's mother. She sat in the seat in front of Lynette, holding Kissy.

Mrs. Lovering stood up so fast, Kissy's neck nearly snapped. "You can't change the rules. That child did not pay a registration fee or fill out an application. And he's a *boy*! He does not belong in this pageant."

"I'd like to see what Rudy Parsley can do," Mr. Randolph said, grandly ignoring her. "What do y'all think?" The audience clapped and cheered their approval.

Bambi's mother sat back down in a huff.

"Okay, Rudy." Mr. Randolph waved him toward the front of the stage. "Tell us what your talent is. I bet it has something to do with that big bag."

"Yep." Rudy set the shiny tote on the floor. Doublewide's seal head poked out. He looked around wildly.

"My talent is my cat, Doublewide the Wonder Cat," Rudy explained. "He can tee-tee in the toilet. And nobody learned him."

"That *is* a talented cat," Mr. Randolph agreed, keeping a straight face. "But how is Doublewide gonna show the folks this amazing feat? You don't happen to have a toilet in that bag, do you?"

Everyone laughed.

"No, but I have this." Rudy wiggled out of the plastic inner tube and set it on the stage floor. "It's kind of like the toilet seat at home."

In the audience, my sister shielded her eyes with one hand. I wished I could disappear myself. Rudy was actually going to set that cat on the inner tube so he'd tinkle in front of everybody!

Mr. Randolph gave the audience an exaggerated wink. He was clearly tickled with Rudy. "Take it away, Rudy and Doublewide!"

Rudy picked up the cat and placed his hind legs on the inner tube. Rudy had pumped too much air into the inner tube and Doublewide's paws kept slipping off. Shoving him back on, Rudy said, "Okay, Doublewide. Pee!"

At that moment, something went *yark!*

Doublewide spotted the dog on Mrs. Lovering's lap. He hissed and his back arched. Then he shot off the stage. As he leaped, his hind toenails punctured the overinflated inner tube, which burst with a loud *pop!* It sounded like a starter pistol.

Kissy squirmed out of Mrs. Lovering's arms and scuttled across the judge's table. Doublewide jumped up on the table, too. Three times Kissy's size, he could have easily flattened the dog with one swat, but Kissy's constant yapping threw him off.

"Get these animals out of here!" the woman judge exclaimed.

"Doublewide!" Rudy yelled. "Come back and finish your trick!"

"*Kissy!*" Bambi screamed.

One of the men judges lunged for Kissy, but the dog squirted away like a bar of soap and chased Doublewide off the table and down the first row of the audience. Some people laughed, but others jerked their feet back or climbed up on their chairs. Doublewide bounded under a parked truck, with Kissy yipping right behind.

Rudy burst into tears. "He's run off again!"

I remembered the night Rudy sleepwalked. It seemed like the things he loved were always leaving him—his father . . . and now that stupid cat. Doublewide had a habit of hitchhiking with strangers. Suppose the cat crawled into the back of one of the trucks and the truck drove off? Rudy would never get over it.

There was only one thing to do. I raced across the stage and vaulted to the ground, my dress sailing up like a parachute.

"Hey, young lady!" said Mr. Randolph. "You have to perform your talent!"

"Go on without me!" I called as I ran across the carnival grounds.

I glimpsed the galloping cat on the other side of the truck. Doublewide was fast, but not as fast as Bambi's dog. His weight slowed him down. And Kissy was gaining.

"Doublewide!"

The cat didn't break stride as he sprang to the ledge of the Pick-Up-Ducks game. He tried to jump over the "creek" of bobbing yellow ducks but didn't quite make it. Kissy leaped up and nipped his tail. There was a huge splash, followed by a *yip*. Plastic ducks and water sprayed everywhere.

I bagged the drenched cat as the guy running the game fished a soggy Yorkie out of the stream. She was no bigger than a damp hamster.

"I believe this is yours?" he said.

"'Fraid so." I clamped Doublewide under one arm and Kissy under the other, but not before they both shook themselves all over me.

By the time I reached the stage, my soaked dress was covered with dust, straw, and fur. I handed Kissy to Bambi's mother then dumped Doublewide in Lynette's lap as I sank into Rudy's empty seat. He was still onstage, standing in one corner.

"How's it going?" I asked.

"Almost finished with the talent part," Lynette said. "Thanks for bringing this wretched animal back."

"I guess Bambi will win," I said regretfully. "Her dress is so pretty."

Miss Odenia sniffed. "Bambi broke the rules. It says on the registration form, 'no pageant attire.' That's a custom-made pageant dress, not an off-the-rack outfit. I bet she'll be disqualified in the appearance category."

My heart lifted, then hit bottom again. If I hadn't run offstage, I might have had a chance. My recitation may have cinched the pageant.

"I'm glad Mama and Daddy aren't here," Lynette said. "Have you lost your mind? Telling the entire county about my holey underpants? Why didn't you say you were going to buy me a new bedroom suite instead? And *what* happened to your eyelashes?"

After I told her the whole sordid story, she sighed. "Honestly, Rebel, could you have done more to lose this pageant?"

"And next we have Miss Bambi!" Mr. Randolph announced after one of the Chanel-Winter-Baylee-Shelbylynn girls finished slaughtering "Tomorrow" from *Annie*. The last shrill notes flew out of her mouth and seemed to land in the rafters of the stage like a flock of starlings. People actually flinched.

Flashing her brilliant smile, Bambi trotted up to the microphone.

Mr. Randolph stood back, as if afraid to get too close to her. Bambi grabbed the microphone from him and chirped, "Hi, y'all! I'm gonna play a little number that my dog Kissy just *loves*. There's Kissy! Isn't she the sweetest li'l thing? 'Yes Sir! That's My Baby' comin' up just for you, Kissy-poo!"

She planted her feet apart and began plucking at the ukulele. The judge's faces didn't give anything away, not even when Bambi flipped the ukulele over her head and played it behind her back. At the end of her song, she dropped into a deep curtsy and skipped back in line to thin applause.

Mr. Randolph spoke. "And last-but-certainly-not-least, we have Miss Lacey Jane. What is your talent, sweetheart?"

Lacey Jane lumbered to the front of the stage. "I sort of made up a dance," she said. "Well . . . maybe it's not really a dance, but I call it that."

She was going through with it!

"Do you want to tell us anything about your—um—dance?" Mr. Randolph asked.

Lacey Jane looked like she was going to keel over in a faint, but she said, "I picked this song because it puts me in mind of my mother. How she's watching over me."

Mr. Randolph nodded at Anita, who switched on the music Miss Odenia brought. Rushing violins whirled from the speakers. Then Patsy Cline's voice cascaded over the audience like a waterfall.

Lacey Jane stood poker-still. I held my breath, waiting for her to start stumbling like a busted puppet.

But Lacey Jane kept her feet nailed to the stage. Instead, she raised her arms over her head and began moving her hands. Her feet never moved, but her fingers performed a ballet. Her fingers sketched every note of music and every word Patsy Cline sang.

I never noticed how graceful Lacey Jane's hands were.

One minute, her hands were swans swimming on a pond, the next, they were roses bursting open in a flutter of petals. Everyone—even Bambi—was hypnotized by the music and her movements.

When the violins rushed in again at the end of the song, Lacey Jane's hands twirled like leaves in a gust of wind, then dropped still by her side. She bowed her head. At first I thought she was hogging the bow, but then I realized she was afraid to look up.

The applause was deafening. My palms burned, I clapped so hard. Lacey Jane took that pretty song and turned it inside out. And she took us along on the ride, all of us rising and falling with every note.

Finally Lacey Jane looked up and gave the audience a small smile. Then she ran to her place in the line.

"Thank you, Miss Lacey Jane," Mr. Randolph said. "In this *most* unusual pageant, we have decided to let Miss Rebel McKenzie perform her talent. C'mon up here, little lady."

Did I hear right? I still had a chance! Lacey Jane was clapping enthusiastically, urging me to come back up onstage.

Seeing Lacey Jane's flushed face made me realize something. She really meant what she said in her interview, and her talent was the best so far. Of us all, she deserved to win the pageant.

I couldn't give my recitation. It was just too darned good. I had to do something else, throw the pageant so

Lacey Jane would win instead of me. What would the judges hate?

"Be right back," I told Mr. Randolph. "I have to get my—uh—prop."

In the tent, I dashed over to the cooler and flung open the lid. I grabbed a can of RC Cola and popped the top. Tipping my head back, I guzzled the soda, swallowing huge air-filled gulps. Then I ran back onstage.

"Miss Rebel, what kind of act are you gonna do?" he asked when I bounced over to him.

I didn't answer. The two glasses of milk I had earlier collided with the RC I'd just chugged. Would those breathing exercises pay off? I sucked in a mouthful of air like an opera singer, opened my mouth, and let 'er rip.

"ConnecticutMassachusettsVirginiaSouthCarolinaNorth CarolinaGeorgiaNewHampshireNewJerseyNewYorkMaryland DelawarePennsylvaniaaaaaaaaaa—"

I was running out of oxygen. My lungs felt like old balloons. Squinching my eyes closed I pretended I was a zeuglodon (the gigantic sea-dwelling mammal) battling a prehistoric shark. The shark pinned me to the rocks, moving in for the kill. The shark could stay underwater longer than me. . . . But wait! There was a tiny bubble of air tucked in one corner of my lungs.

I pushed it out, along with *"RhodeIslaaaaaand!"*

I did it! I finally belched all thirteen colonies! I was so excited, I hugged Mr. Randolph.

"I burped out the thirteenth colony!" I said gleefully.

Then I cut my eyes over at the judges. They were actually laughing! The judges were supposed to be serious. They must have *loathed* my act. I didn't stand a chance.

Mr. Randolph pulled a baby-blue handkerchief from his pocket and mopped his forehead. "Well, folks, we have enjoyed a *variety* of acts today. Let's give Miss Rebel a big hand!"

Not too big, I thought, squelching back to the line.

"That was dis*gust*ing!" Bambi said. "I knew you'd flake out."

Mr. Randolph glanced at the judges. The woman judge held up one finger.

"Folks, our esteemed judges are in a pickle. They are flat-out stumped by the array of beauty and talent here today! They've requested a short intermission so they can discuss the fine qualities of each of these young ladies. Take a break, y'all. I'll holler when they're ready."

Bambi, Lacey Jane, me, and Rudy sprinted off the stage.

Bambi ran immediately over to her mother. "Oh, my poor little Kissy! She's drowned! And it's all that nasty cat's fault!"

"You're welcome," I said acidly.

Lynette gave Doublewide to Rudy. "Whatever possessed you to stuff that cat in my tote bag?" she said. "And drag him out onstage in the middle of the *pageant*?"

"He can do a trick," Rudy said, squeezing his cat. "And it's better than some of the acts I saw."

I couldn't argue with him there. Doublewide peeing on a pretend toilet seat was way more entertaining than hearing "Tomorrow" sung so bad you wished it would never come.

Miss Odenia hugged Lacey Jane. "You did a beautiful job! I took pictures so your father can see how you dazzled everybody."

"Thanks," Lacey Jane said. "But Bambi is still pretty stiff competition."

"We'll see." Miss Odenia gave a mysterious smile.

I looked down at my wet, dirty skirt. Even if Bambi wasn't disqualified for wearing a pageant dress, nothing was as bad as being covered in straw and cat fur. I wouldn't even get last place.

"Folks, may I have your attention!" Mr. Randolph's voice boomed over the loudspeaker. "The judges have reached a decision. Please return to your seats!"

After a scramble, the audience was reseated, and the Violets were once again lined up onstage.

I caught Lacey Jane staring at me, and gave her a salute. With that talent act and her interview, she was a shoo-in.

Mr. Randolph bent down as the woman judge handed him a folded piece of paper. He unfolded it, then looked out at the audience.

"After all that excitement, I can't stand another second

of suspense, can you?" *So get* on *with it*, I wanted to yell. "The judges had a difficult choice. They said it was *very* close between two young ladies. Both gave outstanding performances. But one went beyond the call of duty in conduct befitting—" He stopped, tangled in his own sentence.

Bambi nudged me and smirked. "He's just trying to make one of the other girls feel better. *Not* you."

Making a big show of unfolding the paper and holding it at arm's length in front of his face, Mr. Randolph cleared his throat dramatically.

Then he boomed, "The winner of the third annual Better-Off-Dead Frog Level Volunteer Fire Department's beauty pageant, Violet category *is* . . ."

I held my hand out to Lacey Jane, ready to be the first to shake it.

". . . Rebel McKenzie!"

TWENTY

The Return of Job

I shook my head like I was trying to knock water out of my ears. Did Mr. Randolph just say *my* name?

The Chanel-Winter-Baylee-Shelbylynns squealed and hugged me. One of them jabbed me with her baton, so I know they weren't really thrilled I'd won.

Lacey Jane ran off the stage as soon as my name was announced.

"Wait!" I called after her. "It's a mistake!"

"Darn right it's a mistake," Bambi said, her frozen smile so brittle you could cut glass with it. "I've been robbed!"

Bambi's mother agreed. She stood up and yelled, "I demand an accounting of the judge's scores!"

"Sit down, Mimsie," Miss Odenia said. "Rebel won fair and square."

"C'mon up here, Rebel McKenzie," Mr. Randolph said, beckoning to me.

I walked forward, my knees rubbery. Mrs. Randolph teetered across the stage on her little-bitty feet. Anita followed, carrying my prizes.

"Congratulations, my dear," Mrs. Randolph said, standing on tiptoe to kiss my cheek. Then she handed me a plastic termite.

"Here are your winnings, Rebel McKenzie," Mr. Randolph boomed. "First, a model termite from Better-Off-Dead Pest Control and Bridal Consignment. Remember, folks, when you have bugs or an unused wedding dress, think of us!"

Next, Mrs. Randolph gave me a large pink envelope.

"From those fine people at the 7-Eleven—*Oh, thank Heaven for 7-Eleven!*—a gift certificate for one Slurpee every day for thirty days! And a *check* for two hundred and fifty *dollars!*" Mr. Randolph exclaimed. "What do you think of that, Miss Rebel?"

"Great," I said weakly. If today had been yesterday, I would have snatched the check, run home, and packed my duffel bag for Saltville. Now I felt like Rudy's inner tube after Doublewide clawed it.

"Okay, Mama, do the honors!" Mr. Randolph stepped back.

Mrs. Randolph draped a wide pink ribbon over my shoulder. Printed in red letters was MISS FROG LEVEL VOLUNTEER FIRE DEPARTMENT, VIOLET CATEGORY—SPONSORED BY BETTER-OFF-DEAD PEST CONTROL AND BRID— Apparently the sash writer ran out of room.

Then Mrs. Randolph picked up a glittering rhinestone tiara from the velvet pillow Anita held. She stretched up to put it on my head.

"Miss Frog Level Volunteer Fire Department, Violet Category!" Mr. Randolph bellowed, and everyone clapped again.

And then it was over. The Violets were hustled off-stage so the Roses could make their entrance.

At the bottom of the steps, Bambi got in one last dig. "That tiara doesn't fit you."

"And I suppose it was custom-made for your big fat head?"

Suddenly I was surrounded by people.

"I'm so glad you won!" Viola Sandbanks said. "You put Mimsie Lovering's hoity-toity nose out of joint!"

Palmer Sandbanks threw her arms around me. "Rebel, you made us all so proud! Alvin and me cheered the loudest. Did you hear us?"

When it was Lynette's turn to squash me in a hug, she said, "You always do things your way, don't you? Sometimes it works."

Rudy jumped up and down, tugging my sash. "Rebel—Rebel—Rebel—!"

"What, Rudy?" I said.

He pulled me down to give me a sticky kiss. "You were the best one!"

"Thank you!" I gave him the plastic termite. "I have to go find Lacey Jane."

But Miss Odenia, who'd been standing to one side, said, "Let her go, Rebel."

"But she was so upset! And she should have won, not me! That's why I changed my talent." Tears burned my eyes.

She put her gloved hand on my shoulder. "Come take a walk with me."

Away from the others, I began to cry. "I wanted her to win! I really did!"

"I know," Miss Odenia said. "Lacey Jane knows it, too. She'll be okay, Rebel. That girl has been through a lot, but she's starting to come out the other end. She'll be just fine."

We sat down on a bench by the Ferris wheel. The ride was stopped, and the cars rocked gently. From the very top car we heard a girl shrieking in fear and delight.

"Quit it!" the girl yelled to the boy next to her. "Don't move!" The car swayed, and she laughed.

Miss Odenia tilted her head back, watching them. When the ride shuddered to life again and the cars zoomed toward earth, she smiled.

The tiara slipped, and I reached up to catch it. The combs scratched my scalp. If it wasn't for Miss Odenia, I wouldn't have learned to pivot turn or talk about something besides myself.

I couldn't give Lacey Jane the title of Miss Frog Level Volunteer Fire Department, Violet Category. But maybe—just maybe—I could try to make somebody else happy.

We put Miss Odenia on the noon Greyhound to Richmond. Her friend Ercel Grady would pick her up there and take her to Terrapin Thicket.

Everyone gathered at the bus station in Red Onion—me, Lacey Jane, Rudy, Lynette, Viola Sandbanks, Palmer, Mr. Beechley, Mrs. Maybelline Randolph, and Bambi's mother (Bambi was at a singing lesson).

Miss Odenia kissed each of us twice, then climbed on the bus and took her seat. Her navy gloved hand waved at us through the window till the bus was gone in a cloud of choking brown smoke.

Back at Grandview Estates, we all trooped to the 7-Eleven. I treated everyone to a Slurpee (mine was free). After buying Miss Odenia's bus ticket, paying Mr. Whistle back for the pageant registration fee, and buying eight Slurpees, I had twenty dollars and sixty-one cents left from the prize money.

In the pet section of 7-Eleven, I found a catnip mouse for fifty-nine cents and bought it for the Wonder Cat.

Afterward everyone went their separate ways, leaving me, Lacey Jane, and Rudy with nothing to do. We wandered over to the vacant lot by the sewer pipe.

"I hope Miz Odenia's having a good time," Lacey Jane said. The sun glinted off my tiara. She was using it for a headband.

"She'll be back at the end of the summer," I said, nudging a pebble with the toe of my flip-flop. I thought I saw the imprint of a trilobite, but I was wrong. Miss Odenia would have all kinds of exciting things to tell us when she came home.

I glanced around for Rudy, who was where he wasn't supposed to be, as usual. "Rudy, get away from the sewer!"

"Seee what I founnnnnnnd!" he belched.

"What? Talk right!"

Ever since last night, Rudy couldn't stop burp-talking. His father had finally called. Rudy scampered to the phone, sucked in a deep breath, and burped, *"Hey, Daddy! How's Mud Hooogggg?"*

We could hear Chuck's laughter on the other end. Lynette had said, "Rebel McKenzie! You taught my baby to talk and burp!"

I was giggling too hard to care. Rudy was pretty good! But then, he had learned from the Master.

Now Rudy ran over. He grabbed one of my hands and one of Lacey Jane's and tugged us over to the sewer pipe.

"Looook!"

He pointed at a box turtle scaling a hill of dirt. It was the oldest, most beat-up turtle I'd ever seen. Its legs and neck were leathery as an old suitcase, and its shell was nicked and scarred.

I squatted down. With my keen paleontologist's eye, I made out very faint red marks on the back of the turtle's shell.

"Check this out." With my finger, I traced the ghostly letters.

EG + OM

Lacey Jane stooped so fast, her tiara tipped over one eye. "Rebel! It's Miz Odenia's Marriage Turtle!"

"Job? It can't be."

"It *is*," Lacey Jane insisted. "How did it get here?"

"God brought him on his cloud," Rudy said.

"I doubt it." I touched the turtle's rough shell. His toenails scrabbled in the dirt, trying to get away. "Remember when the trucks brought the carnival rides? They were from Midlothian. Miz Odenia said it was close to Terrapin Thicket."

Lacey Jane sat back on her heels. "The turtle got picked up with the carnival rides. And rode all the way here! But—he's so *old*!"

"I want to keep him!" Rudy said, picking up the turtle. The turtle pulled his head inside his shell but his legs churned like he was swimming in the air.

"No, Rude. Job is going home. Did you forget what my book said?"

Reluctantly, Rudy set the turtle down. The shell

remained closed. "Uh-oh. I musta hurt him."

"He's just waiting for us to go away," I told him.

Lacey Jane looked at me. "You know what this means?"

"Miss Odenia won't be back. Ever." It wasn't scientific, but there was no other explanation. Nothing about this summer had turned out like I'd planned.

"We're still here," Rudy said, as if reading my mind.

"Yep. So we are." I stood up and wiped the sweat from my upper lip. We *were* here. Right now. Today.

The leaves of the trees at the edge of the vacant lot shivered with the faintest stirring of air. Was it?—yes, it was.

The first cool breeze of the summer.

Rudy Vizits God

August 9

Dear Skeeter,

How are you? Cleaned any ditches lately?

Here is your $20. I got it winning a beauty pageant! Can you believe it? That's over, and I'm a paleontologist again (the Ice Age kind, not the dinosaur kind). I'm working on a dig at the sewer pipe. So far I haven't found much. But you never know, do you? Next summer I'm going to the Kids' Ice Age Dig in Saltville.

Rudy (my nephew, yes, I'm an aunt!) is with me. He looks for box turtles. He has a baby one in a pen in the backyard and feeds it hamburger. Doublewide (the cat) stuck his nose in the pen, and the turtle hissed at him! Doublewide jumped a mile. It was so funny!

Lacey Jane (next door neighbor) comes, too. She works on her Girls Without Mothers Club. Right now she is drawing uniforms. All the members will wear pink ball gowns. I myself think that is a bit much. Miss Odenia (another neighbor) was going to be the head one of the club, but she went home. So Lynette (my sister) will run it.

Warning! A girl named Bambi (trouble on a stick)

is coming to your prison! She heard you-all wear navy jumpsuits, which she says is a fashion foe-pa. (That's French for mistake.) Tell the Warden to lock the doors! That girl will make you wish you were never born.

Don't spend the money in one place! Ha-ha! Have a great summer!

Your friend,

Rebel McKenzie

LYNETTE'S FAMOUS HOT DOG SPAGHETTI

Ingredients:

    Small box of spaghetti

    2 or 3 hot dogs

    Half cup of ketchup

    Quarter cup of sugar

    1 can of peas (optional)

Boil the spaghetti until it's done. Slice hot dogs and fry in a skillet. Add cooked spaghetti. Pour ketchup in, enough to coat. Stir sugar in. Add peas if you want. Heat, dish up, and eat!

REBEL'S DELICIOSO RUDY CAKES

Ingredients:
White bread
Margarine
Karo syrup (the light kind)

Toast bread in toaster. Melt margarine in skillet. Add enough syrup to make a gooey mixture. Cook toast on both sides in syrup. Put on a plate. Cut in triangles to make it fancy. Call the hogs to the table!

Acknowledgments

This book began as a present to my sister, a gift wrapped in a mammoth bow to the crazy times we shared when Pat was in beauty school and I was her guinea pig. Then my characters ran off my stage set and it was all I could do to keep up with them.

Many people helped along the way. My agent, Tracey Adams, and everyone at Adams Literary, cheered Rebel on from the start. Emily Meehan, my editor, gave Rebel free rein, and the rest of the folks at Disney-Hyperion guided the book through production with their usual efficiency. Blueberry Slurpees for everybody!

My Hollins University friends laughed at all the right places when I read the first chapter. Their support in my fledgling projects is like a glass of sweet tea on a July day. A giant roll of Necco Wafers goes to Connie Van Hoven, who read the novel to put me out of my misery and pronounced it good. Cheers to Tracey Chesler for letting me steal her hand model experience. And a big thanks to Frank for his encouragement over the years.

Last, for those eagle-eyed readers who have spotted Frog Level on the Virginia map, I borrowed the name of the real town and moved it to suit the story.